ROMANCE IN SLEEPY HOLLOW

MARCIA LYNN McCLURE

Published by Distractions Ink
1290 Mirador Loop N.E.
Rio Rancho, NM 87144

Published by Distractions Ink
©Copyright 2015 by M. Meyers
A.K.A. Marcia Lynn McClure
Cover Photography by © /Dreamstime.com and © /Dreamstime.com
Cover Design and Interior Graphics by Sandy Ann Allred/Timeless Allure

First Printed Edition: December 2015

McClure, Marcia Lynn, 1965—
Romance in Sleepy Hollow: a novella/by Marcia Lynn McClure.

ISBN: 978-0-9970959-0-6

Library of Congress Control Number: 2015920039

Printed in the United States of America

To Stace—

For loving the Legend of Sleepy Hollow with me!
Muchas smooches!

CHAPTER ONE

She was awake. Oh, she was most definitely awake. In fact, Tansy had been awake for some time; she just couldn't resist the desire to lie in her bed and bask in the cool, crisp autumn breeze tenderly wafting in through the open window. It seemed to Tansy that the cherished space of time between summer's scorching heat and winter's thoroughgoing cold, when she could sleep with her windows open all night, was far, far, far too brief. Therefore, each autumn morning, Tansy did indeed linger in her bed for at least half an hour after waking, simply for the sake of savoring the scents, sounds, and chilled, revitalizing breezes of autumn.

Keeping her eyes closed, Tansy sighed with satisfaction. Except for the place where her head rested, her pillowcase was cool—near to cold, in fact—and she loved it! Slipping her feet out from under her warm covers, she was delighted by the cool temperature that met them. Oh, how she loved autumn! All year long she waited for it— well, from December 26 to about mid-August anyway. After all, she loved the holiday season nearly as much as she loved autumn, so it wasn't until just after Christmas Day that Tansy began to miss her favorite time of the year.

Turning over onto her back, Tansy did then open her eyes. The sun hadn't yet peeked over the horizon, but the warm, golden light in the east that preceded it was beginning to glow just above the mountaintops. The morning breeze puffed a somewhat strong breath for just a moment, sending the leaves on the trees swishing their swishing sound and causing another smile to spread across Tansy's face.

"Oh, why can't every morning feel this beautiful?" Tansy sighed aloud. Of course, she knew that if every day of the year was an autumn day—no matter how beautiful it was—it would cease to be as desperately anticipated and as gratefully greeted by the world. Still, it was a thought Tansy often pondered—just as George Eliot had written so long ago—and she quoted aloud, "Delicious autumn! My very soul is wedded to it, and if I were a bird I would fly about the earth seeking the successive autumns."

Tansy sat up in her bed and smiled as she glanced to her nightstand to where a plaque adorned with the same quote sat on a metal easel beneath her lamp. "Delicious autumn!" she repeated.

Not wanting to leave her warm bed or the cool breeze breathing through the window, Tansy stood and began making her bed. As she spread her autumn-themed quilt with its lovely maple leaf pattern over her bed, she glanced up to the vinyl lettering she'd adhered to the wall the year before—the lyrics to one of her favorite vintage songs, "Autumn Leaves."

Tansy giggled to herself, for she knew that dubbing her bedroom "An Autumn Haven," complete with a sign hanging above the door of the entrance, might seem a little too much for anyone else. She knew that the artwork ornamenting the walls in her bedroom—such as a lovely scene of an old farmhouse with pumpkins piled on the porch, a tire swing hanging from a large maple tree bursting with golden leaves in the front yard, and a pile of fallen leaves beneath it—might not appeal to many others. Her bedframe even boasted not only autumn bedding but also metal scrollwork of acorns and leaves imbedded in wood. Sunflower and autumn leaves candle votives sat atop tall candlestick holders embellished with glass insets the colors of autumn—red, orange, gold, and olive green. All the room was autumn, and to Tansy, it didn't matter what anyone else might think, for it was *her* bedroom—her haven, her perpetual place of autumn— and she loved it.

Docking her phone, Tansy chose her Autumn Leaves playlist (composed of fourteen of her favorite versions of the classic song), stripped off her pajamas and undies, and hopped in the shower. She'd spent a little too long enjoying the atmosphere of the calm, cool morning and now would have to hurry if she were going to make it on time to work.

It wasn't easy splitting her time between work at the family apple orchard and fruit stand during the day and then moonlighting late several nights a week all September through October for the cemetery walking tours. Still, Tansy couldn't imagine an autumn without one or the other—or worse, either!

Ever since she was a little girl, Tansy had loved the family apple orchards. She'd literally grown up climbing apple trees, picking apples, and helping prepare the apples for transport and sale. To Tansy, the apple orchard was a piece of heaven on earth, and she was glad that, even though the time had come when apples weren't able to provide enough income to support the family entirely, her father had managed to hang onto the orchards and keep them healthy and producing, even for the fact he'd begun working as a contractor.

Years ago, when she'd been a tweenager, Tansy and her family had visited Washington State. Although it was a beautiful place and although there were apple orchards there, Tansy had been wildly disappointed when the family, while traveling, had begun to see more and more orchards that had been planted with dwarf rootstocks growing on trellises. Using trees barely over eight feet tall most times, this modernized method of producing apples was nearly heartbreaking to Tansy and her family. After all, there were no tall, sturdy tree trunks or limbs to climb on, no difficulty in picking the apples, no ladders needed, and hardly any windfalls. Of course, where producing apples for food was concerned, the method of using dwarf apple trees on trellises made for more volume of fruit with less labor and less disease of the tree.

But it still broke Tansy's heart to see it, and ever since, she'd valued her family's apple orchard all the more. Sure, the Sheridan family orchard wasn't so old as some—certainly not nearly as old as Endicott's 380-plus-years-old pear tree, planted in 1630 and still known to bear fruit. But the Sheridan family's apple orchard was near to one hundred years old and still as healthy and prolific as ever it was—and Tansy loved it. It was why she worked so hard to help keep it going, why she'd chosen to learn about apples, apple orchards, and other fruit-bearing trees instead of getting a regular botanist's degree—for the love of the orchard.

Tansy wasn't at all naïve, however. She knew that one day the orchard would cease producing as well—that she wouldn't always be able to work with the trees she so loved. But Tansy had decided long ago that she would care for her family's apple trees for as long as possible.

And besides, she loved apples! She'd lost track of how many apple crisps she and her mother had baked over the years—to donate to homeless shelters, battered women's shelters, and orphanages—just so that people in neglect or pain could know the warmth and comfort a bite of baked apple, cinnamon, nutmeg, butter, and oats could provide.

Yep, Tansy Sheridan loved many things. But what she loved most, beyond family—autumn and apples.

♥

"Are you doing a cemetery tour tonight, Tansy?" Tansy's mother, Jeanna, asked.

"Yep," Tansy answered. "But just one two-hour lantern tour. I should be home by nine."

Tucking a strand of long brown hair behind one ear, Jeanna smiled and asked, "Ooo! Is that the one where you take them to the receiving vault?"

Tansy nodded. "Yeah," she answered. "It's the only part of the job that freaks me out, you know? It gives me the willies."

Jeanna laughed. "I thought you'd be used to it by now."

Tansy shrugged. "You would think. But it still freaks me out. Probably because they always have Barnabas Collins pop out of the vault, and it startles me every time…even though I know he's coming."

Jeanna handed a banana-nut muffin to her daughter and sat down at one of the chairs at the kitchen table. "I remember my mom telling me about when they were filming *Dark Shadows* around here," she said as Tansy sat down across from her. "It's kind of a goofy show now, but it was big news then, you know?"

Tansy nodded as she peeled the muffin wrapper off her muffin. "I know. But you'd think they could've at least gotten a good-looking guy to play Barnabas. I mean, Dracula types are always supposed to be irresistibly handsome, and that actor…well, he just wasn't my idea of an attractive vampire." She took a bite of her muffin and mumbled, "Mmm! It's still warm! Thanks, Mom."

"You're welcome," Jeanna said. "Well, you're of the Edward Cullen vampire generation," she pointed out to her daughter. "I prefer more of an Angel from *Buffy the Vampire Slayer* vampire, so I hold every vampire to an even higher standard than you do, I suppose, as far as good looks are concerned."

Tansy laughed, knowing exactly what her mother meant. "Well, if it makes you feel any better, I'd take Angel over Edward any day! But that poor dude in *Dark Shadows* from the '70s…yikes!" She took another bite of her muffin. "I can guarantee you, Mom, if it were David Boreanaz jumping out of the receiving vault at Sleepy Hollow cemetery instead of old Mr. Brenden, the groundskeeper…I might just have a totally different response. But the way it is now, Mr. Brenden always manages to make me nearly jump out of my skin!"

"If David Boreanaz were the one jumping out of the receiving vault, *I'd* be in the rotation for guiding some of those walking lantern tours through the cemetery," Jeanna laughed.

Tansy loved her mom—loved that she was so honest and could easily seem like a twenty-something at times rather than the mid-forty-something she really was.

"Mom, you kill me!" Tansy giggled. "What would Daddy say if he could hear you now?"

But Jeanna Sheridan shrugged. "Are you kidding? I had him wearing the Angel man-doo for years during the late '90s! He totally rocked it! *And* he's way better looking than David Boreanaz anyway…and he knows it."

Tansy laughed and finished the last bite of her muffin. "Well, I guess I should cut that old Barnabas Collins a break. Everybody looked pretty homely in the late '60s and '70s."

"True dat!" Jeanna agreed. "It wasn't a very glamorous decade."

"Anyway, Mr. Brenden does a great job as Barnabas Collins," Tansy sighed. "It just startles me every time, so it makes the tour kind of…well, not as much fun to do. That part of it, at least."

"Well, have as much fun as you can, sweetie," Jeanna said to Tansy. "You probably won't be able to work the cemetery tours forever, so enjoy it while you can."

"Oh, I know," Tansy assured her. "Can I have another muffin for the road?"

"Of course, baby," Jeanna said. "Take a couple out to your daddy for me, will you? And don't forget to tell him that the bathroom sink at your place is acting up again too."

"Okay," Tansy said. Taking three muffins from the plate on the kitchen table, Tansy kissed her mother's cheek as she stood to leave. "I'll see you in the orchard in a while?"

"Yep," Jeanna confirmed. "Daddy wants us to get those trees along the east fence line picked before the kindergarten field trips start arriving tomorrow."

Tansy smiled. "I love when the little field trip kids come to pick apples!"

"Me too," Jeanna agreed. "I'm hoping one day one of you kids will get married and get busy having me some grandbabies to pick apples with."

"Yes, Mother," Tansy moaned, rolling her eyes with exaggerated exasperation.

"I'm just saying," Jeanna teased.

"Yes, Mother," Tansy moaned again. Then winking at her mom, she said, "See you later," and left by way of the kitchen door leading to the back porch.

She giggled as she paused to inhale the fresh morning air once more. Her mother was so funny! Always going on and on to Tansy, her sister, and brothers about getting married and providing some grandchildren for her. Her mother always acted like it was just teasing, but Tansy knew her mother was struggling with a big, bad case of empty nest syndrome. She figured a few grandbabies would help to ease her mother's pain of seeing all her own children grown and moved out of the house. But since neither Tansy nor any of her siblings had seemed to find Mr. or Mrs. Right yet, she knew her mom felt as if she were forever treading water in her empty nest.

The fact was that Tansy's parents, Joel and Jeanna Sheridan, were and always had been wonderful parents. Well balanced and firm in their thinking that the family was the center of the universe and children their most cherished possessions as well as their most important responsibility, love, honesty, necessary but never overly hard discipline, and encouragement were her parents' most essential parenting tools. There was never any guilt applied to control Tansy and her siblings, for her parents saw the use of guilt as the one way to destroy self-confidence and self-worth. Therefore, love, laughter, and more love were what most filled the space in the Sheridan home, and Tansy was not only aware of it but also endlessly grateful.

These were her thoughts as she headed for the orchard to start work on picking the trees that lined the east fence line: parents, siblings, love, and the fact that her poor mother was longing for grandchildren. Those thoughts, and the fact that she still couldn't understand why the guy in the old '70s *Dark Shadows* series hadn't at least looked more like David Boreanaz with dark Luke Skywalker hair or something.

♥

"Hey there, Tansy-Tot," Tansy's father greeted as she approached the storage barn.

"Morning, Daddy," Tansy said, smiling. As his eldest daughter walked toward him, Joel Sheridan's smile broadened. Oh, Tansy had been an adorable little girl, made it through middle school without too much gangly goofiness, and graduated high school as a beautiful young lady. But in that moment, Joel was reminded that Tansy was all grown up. She was a woman now—an all-grown-up woman of twenty-one—and as beautiful as her own mother had been at the same age. After all, Tansy was, and always had been, the spitting image of her mother, Jeanna. She owned the same beautiful, long brown hair, the same dark brown eyes, the same small, turned-up nose. Yep, no one could ever doubt she was her mother's daughter.

As she threw her arms around her father's neck, kissing him on the cheek in the process, Joel returned her hug, hanging on just a bit more tightly than usual. He and Jeanna had both been struggling of late, with the fact that all four of their kids were grown up and pretty much out of the nest. Of course, their boys, Devon and Kyle, had been on their own for years. And Joel and Jeanna's youngest, Kathy, was at college. But both boys lived close to home and helped with the orchard as often as possible, and Kathy was home most weekends. Add to that the fact that Tansy rented a little two-bedroom house Joel and Jeanna had bought years before as an investment—well, none of their kids had moved very far from home and were almost always around. Still, not having their little toddlers running around underfoot was something Joel and Jeanna both missed to a nearly heartbreaking state.

"Mom says you want the east line of trees picked out, right?" Tansy asked.

"Yep. We've got the field trips starting tomorrow, and I'd like the teachers to be able to corral the kids more to the west. It's an easier area to pick."

"It is," Tansy agreed. "Mom said she'd be here pretty quick. And are the boys coming?"

"Devon said he'd be over around ten, and Kyle's gonna take the afternoon shift at the fruit stand," Joel explained.

Tansy smiled at her father, though the moisture in his eyes pinched her heart with sympathy for his feelings of getting older and missing his kids. He was so handsome! Tansy and her mother had often talked about how her father had grown more handsome with age. The crow's-feet at the corners of his eyes when he smiled, his salt-and-pepper hair that had once been so black and was now more salt than pepper, his broad shoulders and arms that were still as muscular as they ever had been, even the way his stomach pouched out just the tiniest bit over his belt—all of it was evidence of a man who had worked hard and lived a happy life.

Still, Tansy knew that, for whatever reason, both her parents were a bit more melancholy than usual.

"Mom says to remind you that my bathroom sink is emptying really slowly again," Tansy told him as she picked up a few battered old boxes.

"Yeah, I oughta just replace the pipes under the sink for you," her father sighed. "I'll try to get over there on Friday, all right?"

"Whenever you can, Daddy," Tansy said. "No rush, okay?"

"Friday is good," Joel Sheridan said. "And I'll meet you out at the east fence line here in a little while, honey."

"Okay, Daddy," Tansy said.

As Tansy walked through the Sheridans' orchard toward the east fence line, she thought of the fact that she was glad she wanted to call her father Daddy. It seemed to Tansy that when a woman forever referred to her father as Daddy, it was evidence of something precious—evidence of a father who had loved and protected his daughter during her growing-up years, evidence that he'd spent a lot of time with her and in doing so successfully solidified her confidence and feelings of self-worth. Tansy's father had been her first hero, her protector, her comforter, her playmate, and her loving disciplinarian.

Exhaling a heavy sigh as she reached the trees near the east fence, Tansy dropped her boxes. "That was random," she said aloud to herself. Then, placing her hands on her hips, she gazed up into the highest branches of the nearest apple tree. "Well, let's get you picked, buddy. I'll need time to take a shower and get dressed before my tour tonight, so don't give me any trouble, you hear me?"

Smiling and laughing a bit, Tansy patted the trunk of the old apple tree. "It's okay, Sirus. I'm just kidding with you."

Taking the ladder from its place leaning against the fence, Tansy positioned it beneath old Sirus. Each of the trees in the Sheridans' orchard had a name, and Tansy had grown up learning all of them. She figured it was why she viewed each tree as more a friend than just a tree. She sort of thought of them as the Ents in Tolkien's *Lord of the Rings* and still half expected one of them to start talking to her at any moment. Especially Sirus, for he was the tallest, widest tree in all of the orchard—like the king of the apple trees, in Tansy's mind.

Taking a box and perching it on top of the ladder, Tansy climbed the ladder and then perched herself on a high, sturdy branch where she could still reach the box in order to put apples in it.

"You might want to warn me, Sirus, if you plan on saying anything," she teased aloud. "Otherwise you might startle me and make me fall."

Goose bumps actually broke over Tansy's arms as a sudden brisk breeze moved through the leaves a moment, sounding just as if Sirus were actually responding.

"Don't freak me out like that!" Tansy playfully scolded. Then, taking hold of a particularly delicious-looking apple, Tansy plucked it from its cluster, rubbed it on her shirt, and enjoyed a juicy bite.

"Mmm!" she sighed with contentment. "Good job, Sirus. Really good job!"

Tansy leaned back on her branch, resting against the tree's sturdy trunk. It was a time to be basked in, not rushed through—sitting in the arms of a beautiful old apple tree, with no one around, just listening to the birds that still lingered in warm autumn and the sound of the leaves as the gentle breeze caressed them, the bees buzzing among the few mushy windfalls nestled in the grass below. The beloved aroma of apples filled Tansy's lungs as she lingered in savoring the moment—of apples and of leaves turning from green to gold, of apples, and of the pumpkin patch abundant with round, plump pumpkins waiting to be picked in the field next to the orchard.

Tansy breathed in the scents of the orchard and whispered, "Sirus, it makes sense to me that there are apple trees in heaven, and when we both end up there a long time from now…I hope you'll be willing to let me enjoy another moment like this one with you."

Closing her eyes, Tansy took another bite of Sirus's apple. "Perfect," she breathed.

CHAPTER TWO

"Why, you're looking especially ghoulish tonight, Meredith," Tansy said as her friend approached.

"I know, right?" Meredith chirped, placing her hands on her hips and exaggerating their swing as if she were walking the catwalk. "I got some different makeup from that new Halloween store that opened up, and I think it's going to stay on way better."

"It *does* look good!" Tansy confirmed. Meredith looked more like the lovely ghost of Cornelia Van der Veen than ever before. The new makeup she'd purchased gave her skin a much more pallid appearance and allowed her eyes to appear more pronounced.

"Yeah, I'm hoping the kids won't be as freaked out by me now," Meredith admitted. "That little boy from last week...I just felt so bad for him."

"Well, it wasn't your fault," Tansy soothed her friend. "I explained to his parents that people pretending to be the ghosts of famous people buried in the Sleepy Hollow cemetery would be appearing throughout the tour to tell us about their history. But they assured me he would be fine." Tansy shrugged, adding, "He was eleven years old, after all. Who knew you would freak him out like that? I guess you're just too good at your job."

"Thanks," Meredith said. "But I still feel bad."

"That's because you're sweet," Tansy said. Taking her short red cloak from where it lay over the back of a nearby chair, Tansy swirled it around to her back and secured the tie at the front of her throat.

"And don't you look very Tess Van Tassel-ish tonight," Meredith teased.

"Even with brown hair?" Tansy asked. "And these slippers...I swear! How did a woman's feet not freeze to death in these?"

"I'm sure they wore wooden shoes when it was cold, most being Dutch settlers and all, right?" Meredith offered.

"It makes sense," Tansy agreed. "Maybe I'll pick up a pair at the gift shop in town or something."

"All right, everyone," Mr. Brenden almost shouted as he entered the small room. "Everyone, settle down. And you ghosts best get to your places. We've got quite a crowd out there tonight, especially for a weekday."

Tansy smiled, amused at Mr. Brenden's 1970s hairstyle; his attention to detail when dressing as Barnabas Collins was admirable.

Having noticed her gaze, Mr. Brenden asked, "Do I look all right, Tansy?"

Tansy nodded. "You look very handsome, Barnabas," she said. "I'm sure I'll jump just as high as I ever do when you appear from within the receiving vault tonight," she added.

Mr. Brenden arched one eyebrow with gladness, nodded, and said, "Thanks, Tansy."

Clapping his hands a couple of times, he ordered, "Okay, everybody, let's get this show on the road." Mr. Brenden looked to where Marvin, one of the younger groundskeepers at the cemetery, stood leaning against one wall. "You can go on out and start handing out the lanterns, Marvin. Be sure to try and give them to responsible-looking adults, okay?"

Marvin rolled his eyes, obviously exasperated with the fact that Mr. Brenden felt the need to remind him every tour, even though Marvin had been working with the tour for years.

"Very well then, Tess Van Tassel," Mr. Brenden said to Tansy, "give Marvin a minute to prepare the tour group, and then you can start."

"Yes, sir," Tansy said.

Tansy smiled as she watched Meredith and the other actors of the tour hurry out the back door and toward the cemetery to take their places. The walking cemetery ghost tour was something Tansy had loved as a child, and she was grateful she could actually participate now that she was an adult. After all, she loved her hometown of Sleepy Hollow, New York. Sure, she'd been born in Tarrytown, New York; two years before, the village trustees voted five to zero to officially change the town's name to Sleepy Hollow. But to Tansy, she'd always lived in Sleepy Hollow—always lived in the most wonderful place in all the world, bathed in the most beautiful autumns on earth—and enjoyed the quiet, sleepy, dream-like life of a Sleepy Hollow native.

Branch grinned as he studied the pretty tour guide. She'd introduced herself as Tess Van Tassel and was dressed head to toe in a perfect costume representing Revolutionary America. The young woman was very well spoken, and it was obvious that she not only knew her local history very, very well but also owned a deep love and respect for Sleepy Hollow.

Until he'd been asked to illustrate a new legend of Sleepy Hollow children's book, as well as author and illustrate a new Sleepy Hollow graphic novel, Branch Jackman had never been to the little village of Sleepy Hollow, New York. And as he stood listening to the incredible history of the area—as he stood beneath a grouping of ancient trees a little chilled by the autumn air of the evening—he realized he'd been missing out, for the place was purely captivating!

All around him, everywhere he glanced, he saw inspiration— from the old iron fences to the leaves of the trees that had already begun to turn red, orange, and gold. The old Dutch church and its burying ground adjacent to the Sleepy Hollow cemetery seemed to breathe ideas to Branch's artist's mind, and he knew what he'd be sketching first.

Still, returning his attention to the pretty tour guide standing facing the group of tourists, Branch smiled. *Yep*, he thought. *Looks like I'm going to find inspiration everywhere here.*

Tansy felt a warm blush heat her cheeks as her gaze fell to the tall, totally hot guy standing near the back of the touring group. He smiled at her as their eyes met, and she half expected to see two vampire fangs as part of his dazzlingly white set of teeth. He was truly *that* good-looking—fictional vampire good-looking. So good-looking, in fact, that Tansy was proud of herself for not stumbling over her words as she continued to give her "beginning of our tour" speech.

The guy wore jeans and a blue flannel shirt with his sleeves rolled up to just beneath his elbows. He had short dark hair, a flawlessly chiseled jawline, a square, mildly cleft chin, and shoulders as broad as a barn! He was so her exact idea of a dream man that Tansy quickly glanced around to ensure that there weren't any movie cameras rolling or something. The guy was too good looking to be just a regular Joe out for a stroll with the other tourists.

But Tansy didn't see any news or TV cameras, so she straightened her posture and tried to funnel her focus back to the group of people waiting for the tour to start.

"As you may or may not know, Sleepy Hollow cemetery is the final resting place of not only Washington Irving's earthly remains but also those of many other well-known people. For instance, we'll be visiting the grave of Andrew Carnegie and William Rockefeller, as well as the graves of two brothers, Paul Leicester Ford and Malcolm Webster Ford, who left this life under tragic circumstances when Malcolm went insane and shot his brother Paul before killing himself as well."

Lowering her voice, Tansy felt a mild satisfaction in her presentation when all eyes widened as she said, "Perhaps if we are fortunate this evening, we might just happen upon the ghosts of Paul and Malcolm Ford…for they are known to appear as their specter selves and attempt to explain their histories to those who visit Sleepy Hollow cemetery."

The hot guy in the back grinned with approval, and Tansy nodded to him with thanks.

"Naturally, we'll be visiting many other graves this evening," she continued, "and none more important to Sleepy Hollow's history than Washington Irving. Oh, what an enchantment did he create when he first penned the marvelous story of Ichabod Crane and the Hessian Headless Horseman, hmm?

"So, ladies and gentlemen, I invite you to join me now as we meander—albeit quietly and with respect to those interred here— through Sleepy Hollow cemetery," Tansy said. "Oh, what intrigue of architecture and art we shall find! And again, if you see a spirit specter approach—whether it be the ghost of some wealthy industrialist, a Revolutionary War veteran, or the Headless Horseman himself—remember to hold your tongue and listen to what said ghost may have to tell you…for if we are respectful of the dead interred here, we will have the honor…each of us…of stepping into the receiving vault near the end of our tour—the very vault from whence Barnabas Collins himself arose sometime between 1967 and 1970, having been trapped within for near to 175 years!"

At the thought of Mr. Brenden hiding inside the receiving vault, preparing to suddenly appear and frighten the tourists, Tansy felt the hair on the back of her neck prickle. She wondered why Mr. Brenden always managed to startle her, even when she knew he would be appearing. Exhaling a sigh at being irritated with her own weakness, Tansy turned, held her lantern high above her head, and said, "Now please follow me." Looking over her shoulder, her eyes met those of the tall, gorgeous man in the crowd, and she couldn't help but smile when she added, "But be wary…for we are treading where the dead rest and ghosts are restless."

Branch thoroughly enjoyed the walking cemetery tour—every moment of it. Of course, his favorite moment was when Barnabas Collins himself leapt out from a tree near the receiving vault, startling not only the tour guests but the pretty Tess Van Tassel tour guide too. Branch could tell she'd really been scared too—sincerely. He was sure she knew the old guy was going to jump out and startle everyone. After all, she was the tour guide, and not one of the "ghosts" who had appeared previously to entertain the crowd with tales of murder, wealth, Revolutionary War, and other histories had seemed to surprise the cute little tour guide at all. But when Barnabas

Collins appeared—well, Branch was afraid the young woman's heart was going to leap out of her chest!

It was an awesome cemetery tour—not the first one Branch had been on but definitely the best. The actors who portrayed various ghosts were costumed perfectly for their individual time period. The atmosphere was dark, breezy, and so extra spooky. Branch figured that allowing some of the tour guests to carry lanterns added to the creepiness of the whole thing, because those holding lanterns would often hold their lanterns off to one side of themselves, peering into the darkness at the pallid tombstones surrounding them. The extra but very limited lighting created the mirage that the tombstones were moving somehow—or that the carvings on them were moving, at least. Of course, the thing he liked best about the overall tour was the tour guide. He figured her name wasn't really Tess Van Tassel, and he found himself wanting to know her real name. He figured he'd find a way to glean the information from her if she lingered in drinking hot chocolate and having cookies with the tour group now that the tour was finished.

"That was awesome!" one man said as he took a cookie from a plate Tansy held out to him.

"Thank you," Tansy said sincerely. "I'm so glad you enjoyed it."

"Oh, we did!" a woman said as she joined the man. Looking at the man, she explained, "We attend as many cemetery walking tours as we can. It's kind of our thing together since the kids all left home. And I'm not kidding you, this is one of the best we've ever experienced. And you were wonderful—just wonderful!"

"Well, thank you. Thank you so much!" Tansy responded. She thought that the man and woman looked to be about her own parents' age, and Tansy wondered for a brief instant what her mom and dad would do if and when the orchard ever allotted them any free time together.

"It really was great," a deep, rich voice said.

Tansy turned to her right to see the tall, hot guy standing there, grinning at her.

"Thanks," Tansy managed to respond. "Um…cookie?" she asked, holding the plate of cookies toward him.

"You bet," the hot guy said, chuckling a bit under his breath. "I…um…I did have one question though, if you have time and don't mind."

Tansy shrugged and said, "Ask away!"

"Are you really a Van Tassel?" the hot guy asked.

Hating to disappoint such a gorgeous, alluring guy, Tansy sighed and admitted, "Nope. Not really. I'm just a Sheridan…just Tansy Sheridan. My parents own the Sheridan Orchard just outside of town. You probably saw it when you were driving in."

The hot guy nodded. "Yeah…yeah, I did. It looked awesome. Everything out here is so…so scenic."

Tansy smiled and giggled a bit. "It's one of the things that makes Sleepy Hollow so unique."

"Yeah, plus the history," the hot guy said. "I could probably spend a year here researching and not make a dent in what I'd like to know, right?"

"Probably," Tansy agreed. Silently she wished the hot guy would stay a year—just so she could stare at him!

"Well, you did a great job tonight, Tansy," the hot guy said, "even if you're not a real Van Tassel."

"Thank you, Mr.…" Tansy hinted. She just had to know his name! She felt like she'd never be able to get beyond wondering what his name was if she didn't find out that very minute!"

"Oh, I'm Ranch. Ranch Jackman," he offered.

"Like the salad dressing!" Tansy exclaimed. She wanted to die in the next instant, however. Like the salad dressing? Had she really said that out loud? What a dork! Who in all the world would be stupid enough to compare the hot guy's name to salad dressing?

She was relieved, however, when the hot guy chuckled, obviously more amused than offended. "No, Branch," he kindly corrected. "You know, like a tree branch."

"I'm so sorry!" Tansy apologized, blushing so hard she thought sure her hair would catch fire. "I guess it's been a long night and I'm not hearing so well or something."

But Branch just smiled. "Not a problem. It's actually a common mistake. I just let it go a lot of the time."

Tansy nodded but still felt like such an ignoramus that she couldn't think of anything else to say.

"Anyway, great job tonight. You guys are awesome," Branch said.

"Thank you. I'm glad you enjoyed it. I hope you'll enjoy the rest of your visit…since it does seem that you're just visiting, right?" she ventured.

"Yeah," Branch confirmed—much to Tansy's disappointment. "I'll be here for a while. But yeah, just visiting."

"Well, you enjoy it," Tansy said. "And if you decide you need an apple, some apple cider, or anything…you know where to find it."

Branch nodded, saying, "Sheridan Orchard. Yep. Thanks."

"Have a nice night," Tansy almost sighed.

She watched then as Branch Jackman turned and strode away.

"Hot, hot, hotness!" Meredith said in a lowered voice as she handed Tansy a fresh plate of cookies. "I thought my eyeballs were gonna pop right out of my head when I first saw that guy in the crowd tonight!"

"I know, right?" Tansy agreed.

"Who's the stiff?" Marvin asked, coming to stand near Meredith and Tansy.

"All I know is his name is Branch and he's just visiting," Tansy sighed.

"Ranch? Like the salad dressing?" Marvin asked. "That's a dumb name."

"No…Branch! Like a tree branch," Tansy quietly corrected. She was further disgusted with herself at misunderstanding Branch's name the first time; it meant she was in the same dork league as Marvin Trace.

"Well, *excuse* me!" Marvin teased. "I can't figure out why you girls go all limp-kneed for guys like that."

Tansy and Meredith both stared at Marvin with expressions of repugnance for a moment before Meredith finally said, "Oh, you mean tall, dark, handsome, and *polite*? Gee, I can't imagine why either." Rolling her eyes with exasperation, Meredith walked away with the near empty plate of cookies she'd traded Tansy for the full one.

"She gets so impatient with me," Marvin mumbled, shaking his head with discouragement.

"Well, quit being a nosy dork, and maybe she'll relax a little around you," Tansy kindly suggested. She knew Marvin liked Meredith—really liked her. And in that moment, she felt sorry for him—because she was pretty sure he didn't have a chance with their friend Meredith.

Turning her attention back to the tour group crowd that was now thinning out, Tansy scanned the lingerers for Branch Jackman. She exhaled a heavy sigh of disappointment—because he was gone. He'd vanished into the night almost as if he'd never been there at all.

♥

"No, Mom, I'm totally serious. He was gorgeous!" Tansy told her mother. Taking a bite of warm apple crisp and cold vanilla ice cream, she mumbled, "Like…spine-tinglingly gorgeous!"

"Mmmm! Spine-tinglingly gorgeous?" Jeanna Sheridan asked. Taking a bite of apple crisp and vanilla ice cream out of her own dessert bowl, she added, "That's pretty gorgeous!"

"I know, right?" Tansy giggled.

"And other than the appearance of this spine-tinglingly gorgeous stranger, how did the tour go?" Jeanna asked.

"Really well," Tansy answered. "Mr. Brenden was in especially fine form as Barnabas tonight." She smiled, remembering how pleased Mr. Brenden had been when she'd complimented him. "I can tell the weather is changing though," she added. "I'm definitely going to be wearing a ton of layers under my costume by Halloween."

"Yes, you are! Because I don't want my baby catching pneumonia," her mother remarked.

Tansy smiled and took another bite of her mother's delicious apple crisp. "Mom, I swear, you and Grandma make the best apple crisp in the world!" she chirped.

Jeanna laughed. "Oh, that's because it's late, and you're tired, and because it's still so warm," she assured her daughter.

"Well, I think it's just because you and Grandma make the best. The fact that I'm tired only makes it better," Tansy said.

"Well, thank you, sweetie," Jeanna said, reaching over and squeezing Tansy's hand with affection. "And, oh! That reminds me. Your daddy went over after he finished in the orchard and fixed your bathroom sink this evening."

"He did?" Tansy asked, feeling guilty. Her daddy worked so hard every day with his contracting business and with the orchard. She felt awful that he'd fixed her sink too. "I didn't mean he had to do it today."

"Oh, he knew that," Jeanna assured Tansy. "He just wanted to do it while he was thinking about it, you know?" Jeanna smiled and laughed a little then.

"What's so funny?" Tansy asked.

Jeanna shook her head, still smiling. "Your daddy," she answered. "I remember when he wouldn't eat anything sweet…seriously, anything. Other than the occasional bowl of ice cream, your daddy was Mr. Healthy for years. But tonight—and don't tell him I told you this—he sat down and ate half of this apple crisp all by himself! *With* ice cream too! And then he'll wonder why he weighs more in the morning."

Tansy giggled. "Daddy is so funny," she offered, "because he'll claim that there was no way he ate half of the apple crisp. He'll blame it on me or you or someone, but he'll never admit to eating that much of something sweet."

"I know," Jeanna laughed. "I love that about him—his moments of ridiculous denial. They crack me up."

"Me too," Tansy agreed.

For a few moments, she and her mother just sat enjoying the warm apple crisp coupled with cold vanilla ice cream—sat enjoying the cozy autumn atmosphere in the kitchen and simply being in one another's company.

"Delicious autumn," Tansy sighed.

"My soul is wedded to it," Jeanna continued.

"I wish my soul were wedded to that hot guy from the tour tonight too," Tansy mumbled playfully.

"I bet!" her mother said. "Being that he was spine-tinglingly gorgeous and all."

"Spine-tinglingly," Tansy laughed.

She savored her next bite of apple crisp and ice cream—vowing to remember that comfortable, picturesque moment spent with her mother for the rest of her life.

CHAPTER THREE

Branch sat down beneath the large maple tree just outside the Sleepy Hollow cemetery fence. He figured it was as good a place as any to begin making rough sketches. The truth was, just about anywhere in Sleepy Hollow seemed ripe with visual inspiration. When he'd left his hotel room that morning in search of a place to begin sketching, he'd found himself somewhat overwhelmed with the abundance of incredible things, places, and people to draw.

Therefore, after walking around for about forty minutes and finding himself back at the Sleepy Hollow cemetery he'd toured the night before, he'd decided to start with some graveyard scenes—old tombstones, ancient trees, the Old Dutch Church off in the distance. Branch figured he could probably spend most of the day just in that one spot, if it weren't for the fact that he knew his butt would start going numb. Still, he readied his sketchpad and pencil and began to draw.

"Cool fence," he mumbled to himself as he began to sketch the ancient wrought-iron fencing across the street. Branch liked old fences. To him it was simply fascinating to think on what an old fence had seen over its long life. And this fence was particularly interesting, being that it had stood in Sleepy Hollow for who knew how many decades upon decades.

"Hi there," a woman's voice said.

Branch looked up to see the woman who had managed to approach him without his noticing. He felt a smile spread across his face when he recognized the pretty young woman from the cemetery tour he'd taken the night before.

"Why, if it isn't Miss Tess Van Tassel herself," he greeted. Quickly he stood and offered her his hand.

She blushed and said, "Oh, I didn't mean to bother you, Mr. Jackman. I was just in town picking up some stuff for my mom, and I saw you sitting over here drawing…and thought I'd just say hi."

She did take his hand, however, and Branch was impressed with the firm handshake she gave him, even though her hands were so small and soft compared with his.

"Well, I'm glad you did, and you're not bothering me at all. I'm just getting started on some rough sketches," Branch explained.

Branch couldn't help but study Tansy from head to toe—for she wasn't wearing a costume as she had been the night before, of course, and he thought she looked even hotter wearing jeans, tiny little woman-sized well-worn work boots, and a red "Sheridan Orchard" T-shirt.

Glancing at the sketchpad he still held, Tansy smiled. "Oh, you're doing the fence! I love that old fence!" she exclaimed. "I always wonder what stories it could tell if it could talk, you know? Like what kinds of historical events, or even everyday events, it's witnessed over its long life."

Branch's smile broadened. "I know what you mean. I suppose it's kind of why I have a thing for fences. I don't think I've ever illustrated one book without some sort of fence in it." He nodded, with raised eyebrows, realizing aloud, "Don't think any of my graphic novels are missing a fence either. Hmmm. I never thought of that before."

"Really?" Tansy asked. "Yep, you must have a thing for fences." She paused a moment and then continued, "How many books and graphic novels have you worked on?"

Branch shrugged. "Enough to make a living," he answered. Smiling at her, he added, "But not so many that I'm eating off solid gold plates, you know what I mean?"

Tansy laughed, and the sound made Branch feel as dazzled as a child on Christmas morning for some reason.

"So you illustrate…like, what? Book covers and stuff?" she inquired.

Branch nodded. "Yeah, mostly children's books—you know, picture books. You're probably a little old to have seen any of my work though."

"Not at all!" Tansy exclaimed, however. "I love children's books! I actually collect them—in moderation, of course. I really love ones with gorgeous illustrations as well as wonderful text! So, you see, I might very well know some of your work."

She smiled at him, and again Branch was transported back to the Christmas morning feelings of his childhood for a moment.

"Okay then, let's see. Have you ever heard of Windy Lyrant?" he asked. He was doubtful Tansy had ever read Windy's work. But Windy was the best selling author of children's fiction he'd worked with, so he figured he'd drop her name first.

To his astonishment, Tansy squealed, clapped her hands together, and chirped, "Of course! I love her books! She's one of my favorite authors. Oh, I just loved her *Pumpkins for Sale* book that was new a few years back. Oh, and that one from last year, *October Breezes*—awesome author! And her illustrators are the best!"

Branch chuckled. "Are they?" he teased. "So…do you remember who the *October Breezes* illustrator was?"

Tansy grimaced, and Branch was amused by the way she wrinkled her nose when she did; it was adorable.

"No, I don't," she admitted. "But I loved the illustrations all the same."

"Well, do you own the book?" he asked.

"Yeah," Tansy answered.

He smiled and said, "Why don't you look and see who illustrated that for Windy when you get home today? You might recognize the name, now that you and I have met."

Branch watched, entirely amused as Tansy's pretty brown eyes widened with understanding. "Branch Jackman?" she breathed. "Oh my heck, that's it! I remember it now—illustrated by Branch Jackman! I cannot believe I didn't put that together last night when you told me your name."

Branch chuckled. "Well, you did think I was named after salad dressing at first. So I suppose it's understandable that my name didn't ring a bell as an illustrator."

"Don't remind me of what a total dork I am sometimes," she sighed as she began to blush.

"I'm just kidding you," Branch told her. "No one remembers the illustrator of a book, so don't feel bad. I actually prefer that people don't know who I am—or rather what I do. It allows me anonymity, and believe me, I relish that."

"Still," Tansy said, "you'd think I would've remembered the name of the illustrator of *October Breezes*, being that I loved the illustrations so much. They're incredible! I even bought an extra copy and had a couple of the illustrations framed for my house."

"Really?" Branch asked, feeling unusually flattered for some reason.

Tansy nodded. "You bet! They're gorgeous!"

"Wow. Thanks," Branch gratefully offered.

A cute little frown puckered Tansy's brows then, and she asked, "So…you say you're also here to work on a graphic novel version of the legend of Sleepy Hollow?"

"Yep," Branch confirmed.

"Like, a gory, bloody, zombie version?" she ventured.

Branch laughed. "No, not at all. I don't do gore…well, at least not much—not like the stuff that's coming out now with the zombie craze in full swing, you know? I do more, like—I don't know—I'll be doing the story, abridging the text into my own words, with art that's…well, I'm going for spooky and atmosphere, but not walking corpses with shreds of flesh hanging from their limbs. Does that make sense?"

"Yeah, it does," Tansy answered. Though in truth, she wasn't quite sure what Branch was trying to describe, so she asked, "Have you got any other graphic non-zombie-type stuff in print that I could order and read?"

Branch smiled but looked almost embarrassed.

"Well, yeah, but I'm not really sure it's your thing, you know?" he answered. "After all, you like children's literature, and mine's more, you know, comic book type stuff."

"No, no! I'm sure I'll love it," she reassured him.

Branch raked a hand back through his dark hair, sighed, and said, "Well, I did a version of *1,001 Arabian Nights* that was released the first of the year. It's probably the only one you would enjoy, if you enjoyed any of my stuff at all."

"Ooo! Sounds intriguing," Tansy said. "I'll order it online today when I get finished with work—rather, tonight when I get finished with my cemetery tour, that is. But for now, I'd better let you get back to *your* work, and I'd better get back to the orchard. We're pressing cider today and tomorrow—you know, just in case you run out of things to draw and feel like indulging in some refreshing, and also very fresh, apple cider."

Tansy knew it was probably a little too forward of her—to invite a near stranger to visit the orchard on the pretext of trying some apple cider—but she couldn't help it. She was really, really, really drawn to Branch Jackman. Of course, she figured every woman on the face of the earth would be drawn to him; he was spine-tinglingly good-looking, after all. Still, it wasn't just the fact that he was so hot. She liked *him*. He was good-natured, friendly, and obviously talented.

"I might take you up on that offer," Branch said, redirecting Tansy's attention away from mooning over him and back to their conversation.

"I hope you do," Tansy said. Nudging his arm with one of her elbows, she mumbled, "I might even be able to hook you up with one of these babies." Gesturing to the Sheridan Orchard T-shirt she wore, she winked at him, adding, "I know a guy."

Tansy was thrilled when Branch chuckled. She'd managed to amuse him, and she figured it was a good sign that he wasn't totally grossed out by her, at least.

"All right then," he said. "That might be worth the trip in itself," he teased.

Still, Tansy felt ridiculous for having even tried to coax him out to the orchard. Could she have been any more obvious in revealing her interest in him? Aside from reaching up to take his face in her hands and kissing him, she thought not.

"Seriously, just if you get bored or something," she explained. "I'm sure you have plenty to do—but if you need a break, you know?"

Oh, she was too cute! Branch knew Tansy was feeling awkward about suggesting he visit her family's orchard, but he thought it was awesome that she had.

"Oh, I know. You tour guide types are always taking care of us tourist types," he said, "making sure we're enjoying your environment and stuff. So thanks for the offer. And I do like apple cider."

Tansy exhaled a quiet sigh, and Branch was glad he'd been able to ease her mind.

"So you're doing another cemetery tour tonight, huh?" he prodded.

"Yeah," she confirmed. "The latest one—ten to midnight. Ugh."

"Well, I might just have to take that tour again," Branch offered.

"Really?" Tansy asked, her dainty eyebrows peaking in surprise. "Why would you want to do that?"

"It was very informative, for one thing," Branch explained. "Historically, you know? And the mood—walking through an old, old cemetery at night with just a few lanterns to light the way? Awesome! It's totally one of the moods I want in the graphic piece I'm working on."

"Yeah, but it's twenty bucks a ticket," Tansy pointed out.

Branch shrugged. "I'll expense it," he said. And then he said something that astonished him. "And you know what else? If you happen to have any free time during the day sometime, would you mind maybe showing me some other local haunts that might work to inspire me?"

"Me?" Tansy asked. "I'd love to show you around Sleepy Hollow!"

Branch could tell by the blush that rose to her face that she was very pleased he'd suggested she help him. It eased his mind, knowing that she obviously wasn't too averse to him, at least.

Tansy could feel that she was blushing, but she couldn't help it. The idea—the mere prospect of the possibility of showing Branch around town in order to spend time with him—was exhilarating!

And then it got even better, for Branch asked, "Would you mind giving me your number so I can call you and see if you really can fit me into your busy apple cider slash cemetery tour schedule?"

"Oh…oh, of course," Tansy stammered.

Branch took his phone out of his pocket, swiped the screen, and said, "Okay, ready."

He handed the phone to Tansy, and she quickly entered her name and number into his contact list.

Then reaching into her own pocket, she retrieved her phone, swiped the screen, and handed it to Branch. "Would you mind putting yours in…so that I know who's calling if you do call?"

Branch smiled, took her phone, and began entering his information. "You mean, *when* I call," he said.

Tansy smiled with elation at his reassurance that he did mean to call her.

"I just hope you can fit me in sometime," he said. "You seem to be pretty busy."

"Oh, I have time," Tansy assured him.

"Okay then," Branch said, handing Tansy's phone back to her and accepting his as she offered it. "Have a good day with your cider and all."

Tansy giggled. "I will. And you have a good day with your drawing and all."

"I'll do it," he said.

"Okay, bye," Tansy awkwardly offered.

"See you later," Branch responded.

Tansy turned, exhaling a heavy breath—only then realizing she'd been breathing unevenly the whole time she'd been talking to Branch. She looked up and began walking toward where she'd parked her car.

When she'd left her parents' home that morning to run some errands for her mom, Tansy had hoped for a miracle, in that she might get to set eyes on the handsome Branch Jackman again. And there he'd been, just sitting under a tree across from the cemetery, almost as if he'd been waiting for her. Of course, Tansy knew he hadn't been just waiting for her, but it was strangely fortuitous all the same. And now his phone even had her name and number saved in it. And even more astonishing was that his name and number were in her phone!

"Okay, I believe in miracles more than ever now," Tansy mumbled to herself as she hurried back to her car. "More than ever!"

♥

"Tanz," Devon hollered up to Tansy.

"What?" Tansy called down from her perch in Abigail's branches.

"There's some guy here, up at the fruit stand," Devon explained. "He says you told him our apple cider was worth coming out here for, but I get the feeling he isn't here for the cider…if you know what I mean."

Tansy's heart leapt with excitement. "Sorry, Abigail, old girl," she said to the apple tree as she began climbing down. "I'll be back to pick you over some more later."

As Tansy hopped down from the ladder, pulling off her gloves and smoothing back her ponytail, Devon chuckled and said, "I was afraid you were gonna break your neck coming out of that tree so fast. I guess you know this guy better than I thought."

"Not really," Tansy admitted. "But you saw him, right? Have you ever seen a hotter guy in all your life?"

Devon smiled, winked at his sister, and said, "Only every morning when I look in the mirror."

"Oh, you're pathetic," Tansy giggled. "Come on," she said, playfully smacking Devon on the arm. "Let's hurry before he changes his mind and gets away."

"Gets away?" Devon laughed. "You'd think he was a greased pig or something."

"Oh, be quiet and come on," Tansy said, "unless you'd rather finish picking Abigail."

"Nope," Devon said, taking off his cap and raking a hand back through his brown hair. "This I gotta see."

"What do you have to see?" Tansy asked.

"You trying to catch a greased pig," Devon teased.

When Tansy arrived at the fruit stand, it was to see her mother and father, as well as her brother Kyle, all standing around Branch. Branch was holding a pint jar full of fresh cider and nodding as he listened to whatever her father was saying at the moment.

"Oh, here she comes!" Tansy's mom exclaimed as Tansy approached.

"Hi, Branch," Tansy greeted.

Branch held up his pint jar of cider and said, "I decided to take you up on your offer and try some Sheridan Orchard cider. It's awesome!"

"Oh, I'm glad you like it," Tansy said.

"Branch here has been telling us that he's in town to work on some book illustrations and whatnot," Tansy's father said. "Sounds like your cemetery tour really inspired him last night."

Tansy's father winked at her with understanding suspicion, and Tansy tried not to blush.

"Yeah, it was a particularly good tour group," Tansy responded. She felt awkward—for not only was Branch smiling at her, but every member of her family was staring at her with all-knowing smiles spread across their faces.

"Daddy, do you think you have a T-shirt that might fit Branch?" Tansy asked her father. "I figured we can pawn one off on him and maybe get some free advertising around town."

"Of course!" Joel Sheridan said. Looking to Branch, he asked, "What size? A large, maybe?"

"That'd be great," Branch said. "But you'll have to let me pay for it."

"Nonsense," Jeanna exclaimed. "We usually just wear them ourselves—you know, an obvious pitch for the orchard." Turning to her husband, Jeanna added, "Bring him a red one, honey. Women love red on a man."

"Red it is," Joel said as he turned and headed for the nearby storage shed.

"Do they?" Branch asked, a slight chuckle escaping his throat.

"Oh, absolutely!" Jeanna assured him. "Ask Tansy. She'll tell you."

"Red, huh?" Branch asked, grinning with mischief.

Tansy felt her cheeks grow pink with embarrassment. "Yep. Women like red on a guy."

"Dude!" Kyle exclaimed, slapping his brother on the arm with the back of one hand. "Did you know that?"

"Nope," Devon admitted.

Turning to his mom then, Kyle asked, "Well, why didn't you ever tell us that, Mom? Don't you think that might have come in handy for me and Devon?"

"I have told you that…both of you! And probably a million times," Jeanna sighed. "But you're both so stuck on blue, you don't hear me."

"I like blue too," Branch interjected. "But if red is what the honeys prefer…" He winked at Tansy, and she felt her blush deepen.

Her family could be so embarrassing sometimes!

"Here you go," Joel said as he returned from the shed. "One Sheridan Orchard T-shirt, size large, and in red so the women will go wild."

"Daddy," Tansy scolded.

"Oh, that's right," Joel said. "Maybe Tansy doesn't want all the women going wild. Maybe she's saving you for herself, Branch."

As Tansy's face burst into a shade of crimson that made her ears burn, she scolded, "Daddy! Knock it off!" as everyone, even Branch, laughed. "The poor man just came for some cider. Sheesh!"

"So are you finding lots of ideas in Sleepy Hollow…for your art, I mean?" Jeanna asked, coming to Tansy's rescue.

"I am," Branch affirmed. "And I asked Tansy if she could maybe find some time to show me some places that she's familiar with that might give me some ideas. I just hope she can fit me into her schedule somewhere."

Branch smiled at Tansy, and she gritted her teeth when Kyle mumbled, "Oh, believe me, she'll fit you into her schedule all right."

"That's a great idea!" Joel exclaimed. "In fact," he began, turning to Tansy, "why don't you take tomorrow off from the orchard? Devon and Kyle will be here all day. That way you can show Branch here some of the less traveled, more remote, and undisturbed haunts in Sleepy Hollow."

"That would be awesome, Mr. Sheridan," Branch said before Tansy even had a chance to respond. "That's exactly what I'm looking for—places the locals know about that maybe aren't so overrun with tourists…even though I, myself, am a tourist."

"Yes, Tanz," Jeanna encouraged. "We'll be fine without you tomorrow. We'll just be pressing cider all day long anyway."

"Would you mind?" Branch asked. "I mean, I don't want to mess up your paycheck or anything, but I really could use a local's knowledge of the area."

"Well, if you're sure you need me to show you around…I'd be more than happy to," Tansy assured him.

Her heart was racing inside her chest! She even felt her hands and legs begin to tremble with anticipation. She was going to spend more time with Branch—alone time with him! It was kind of hard to take in, for it really did seem surreal.

"Awesome!" Branch said. "I, um…I kind of need to see things throughout the day—morning light, noon, evening. Do you think you could maybe help with that, for that long?"

"Oh, absolutely," Tansy answered, almost breathlessly.

"Thanks," Branch said. Then offering a hand to Tansy's father, he added, "And thanks for giving her the time off, Mr. Sheridan. It will be an immense help to me, having a local show me around."

"I'm sure it will be," Joel said. As Branch turned to shake Jeanna's hand, Tansy shook her head at her father in a scolding manner when he winked at her and then arched his eyebrows several times in succession to indicate that he knew she was thrilled to be able to go with Branch.

"Thank you, Mrs. Sheridan," Branch said to Tansy's mom. "The cider was excellent! The best I've ever had. And thanks for the tip about wearing red too. That should come in handy."

"It'll probably come in handy tomorrow," Devon mumbled to Kyle.

Tansy glared at both her brothers, but they only grinned with amusement at her expense.

Turning to Tansy, Branch drank the last bit of cider from the pint jar her mother had given him and then offered it to Tansy.

"Want me just to pick you up right here tomorrow morning?" he asked.

"Sure," Tansy answered.

"Great. What time?"

"Nine?" Tansy asked.

"Perfect," Branch said. "Oh, and I will be going to your late tour tonight again. That tour is awesome! I'll see you there?"

"Yep. I'll be the one pretending to be a Van Tassel," Tansy told him.

"Okay. See you later. It was nice meeting all of you too," Branch said before he turned to head back toward his rental car.

Every one of the Sheridans called bye as Branch walked away.

"The dude rented a pretty nice car, hmm?" Devon said under his breath.

"A black Dodge Charger?" Kyle commented.

"With tinted windows," Devon added.

"Maybe he's dealing," Kyle offered.

"Shut up!" Tansy scolded in a whisper. "You guys are awful! Just wait until one of you brings a girl by the orchard sometime. I've been saving up my own verbal ammunition for years!"

Seeming to ignore their sister, however, Devon and Kyle exchanged glances.

Devon looked to Tansy and teased, "I'll give you this, Tanz. That's the fastest capture of a greased pig I've ever seen."

Rolling her eyes with exasperation at her brothers, Tansy turned to her mom and asked, "Well? Was I exaggerating last night?"

"Not at all!" Jeanna giggled. "Spine-tinglingly!"

As Tansy and her mother had a good laugh over the secret they shared via their conversation the night before, Joel said, "I always wondered why your mom was so determined to dress me in red all the time."

"Dad," Kyle began then, "you got any more T-shirts in red in the shed there?"

"Yeah. I want one too," Devon said.

"Oh, now you're willing to advertise the orchard, hmm?" Joel chuckled.

"Well, yeah. If the chicks really do dig red, I'm all in!" Devon said as he and his brother bumped knuckles.

Jeanna Sheridan shook her head as she watched her husband and two sons head for the storage shed.

"They're ridiculous, Mommy," Tansy giggled.

"I know. Oh, I know," Jeanna laughed.

Then holding out the pint jar Branch had handed to her, Jeanna offered it to Tansy. "Now, when I was dating your daddy, I would've filled up this jar with some cider and drunk it right away...just so I could drink after him. It's so intimate, after all."

"Mother!" Tansy exclaimed. "That is so…well, it's gross, if nothing else." Secretly, however, Tansy wasn't as shocked as she pretended to be. In fact, the more she thought about it, the more she kind of liked the idea.

"Go ahead, sweetie," Jeanna encouraged in a whisper. "After all, it'll almost be like kissing him, right?"

Still, even as she poured fresh cider into the pint jar, Tansy shook her head and said, "Sometimes I cannot believe the stuff you come up with."

"Be sure to drink all around the rim, Tanz…you know, to make sure you swap some DNA with him," Jeanna instructed.

"Mom!" Tansy exclaimed, giggling.

"Just do it," Jeanna demanded.

Smiling at her mother and shaking her head once more at her mom's even conceiving such a thought, Tansy was no less than deliciously thrilled as she drank cider from the pint jar Branch had drunk from. She was surprised when she actually did feel a thrill of delight race over her spine.

"Well? How does his DNA taste?" Jeanna teased.

"Exquisite!" Tansy laughed. "Absolutely exquisite!"

CHAPTER FOUR

Tansy couldn't keep from smiling every time she glanced at Branch standing in the tour crowd—because every time she glanced at him, he was smiling at *her*. She found it difficult to focus on what she was saying and even stumbled over her words several times while giving her opening spiel. It was like Branch's eyes had a way of reading her mind—or like he had Superman's X-ray vision or something. At least that's how Tansy felt every time she glanced to see him staring at her with an amused grin. He was so stinking handsome! Tansy fancied that he almost looked so fictionally handsome, she wondered if some of the other women in the tour group thought he was a ghost or something—for they all kept stealing quick looks at Branch, and their faces expressed awed skepticism at his existence. Tansy knew exactly how they felt. Yet this was her fourth time being in Branch's presence, and he was nothing if not alive and real—and freaking gorgeous!

The tour was going well (even for Tansy's uncharacteristic stammering here and there), and Tansy found herself wishing it were longer than two hours. She'd take a tour through the cemetery all night long if it meant Branch would be there every time she scanned the tour group. It was an uneventful tour, as most tours were. Meredith was in fine form, playing her ghostly colonial character perfectly. Tansy thought Meredith was even a little too dramatic if anything—and knowing Meredith as she did, she figured her friend's extra special performance was for Branch's sake. After all, Meredith had whistled quietly under her breath to Tansy when she'd seen Branch waiting with the tourists before the tour began. And besides, Meredith was as boy-crazy—or, rather, man-crazy—as any woman Tansy had ever known. Yep, her stellar performance was for Branch's sake, and the fact had almost made Tansy laugh out loud.

Uneventful as the tour had been, something strange did happen as Tansy began to lead the group toward the receiving vault—preparing herself, as always, for Mr. Brenden to leap out and startle the wits out of everyone (especially Tansy).

"What's that over there?" someone in the group asked.

"Pardon me?" Tansy asked, stopping her slow pace toward the receiving vault and turning to respond to the question.

"Over there," one woman said.

The woman was standing near the back of the group, holding the lantern she'd been given high above her head. "Right back there behind that tree. What is that?"

Holding her own lantern a little higher, Tansy walked to the back of the group, stopping next to Branch. Branch held his lantern higher, as well, and with the extra light glimmering over the cemetery grounds then, Tansy could see something she didn't recognize. It looked like a huge mound of dirt, and it puzzled her—for there had never been a mound there before.

"Oh, I, um…I think that's the grave of Anouk Van der Veen," Tansy answered. "She…um…she was the subject of speculation after her death…being that it's said she was buried in a porcelain coffin, with a set of emerald jewels her husband had gifted her at their marriage," she began to explain. "But I don't know why—"

"It looks like someone's disturbed a grave," a man from the crowd suggested.

"Oh, I'm sure it's fine," Tansy said. "The cemetery is well looked after and—"

But before she'd even finished her sentence, the tour crowd had turned as a group and had begun heading toward Anouk Van der Veen's gravesite.

"I'm thinking I better get ahead of this," Tansy mumbled.

"I'll help you," Branch said.

Tansy was so focused on crowd control that she didn't have time to enjoy the fact that Branch had taken hold of her arm in an effort to help hurry her toward the front of the crowed.

"Please, everyone," Tansy said in a raised voice, for the crowd had begun talking amongst themselves. "Let's slow down. We can certainly visit Anouk's gravesite, but let's do it quietly and with respect for the spirits that may be visiting the cemetery tonight."

Upon Tansy's mention of possible ghosts being around—which was, of course, just a ploy to settle the crowd—everyone immediately fell silent.

"Let me just get ahead of you all here and see what exactly is going on," Tansy said.

Once she and Branch had reached the front of the tour group, Tansy turned to the group and said, "Wait here just for a moment while I make certain we have a clear path to visit Anouk, all right?"

Everyone in the crowd nodded agreement, and Tansy almost burst into giggles as everyone's eyes widened to the size of white china saucers with nervous anticipation.

"Would you mind coming with me?" Tansy asked Branch in a whisper.

"Not at all," he assured her, still holding her arm.

The mound of dirt near Anouk's grave was even larger up close. "What in the world is going on?" Tansy asked as she began to hurry closer to the mound of dirt.

She took another step forward, but her foot found no solid ground, and she began to slip.

"Oops! Careful," Branch said as he caught hold of her around the waist with his free hand—but only after he'd dropped his lantern into Anouk Van der Veen's open grave.

Several of the tourists gasped or yelped with being startled, and the entire group rushed forward.

"Damn," Branch mumbled as he stood next to Tansy, staring down into the open grave. Miraculously, the lantern Branch had dropped in order to keep Tansy from falling directly into the grave hadn't broken. Thus it eerily illuminated what lay inside—a shattered porcelain coffin and a woman's skeleton, still wearing an emerald necklace, bracelet, ring, and even lingering shreds of a once-elegant gown.

What shocked Tansy most, however, was the large, roughly whittled wooden stake that had been plunged into the skeleton just where her heart would once have been.

"Wow!" one man exclaimed as he stared down into the open grave. "You guys really know how to put on a show out here, huh?"

Branch looked to Tansy and shrugged slightly.

"We…we try," Tansy said.

An audible sigh of relief exhausted from the tour group as a whole, and Tansy forced a smile.

Whispering to Branch, she said, "Would you mind going to inform someone about this while I redirect the group please?"

"Not at all," Branch answered in a whisper. "As soon as you step away from the open grave, ma'am," he added, taking her arm again and pulling her further away from the deep hole behind her.

"So Anouk Van der Veen," one woman in the crowd began, "was she really buried in a porcelain coffin?"

"Mmm hmm," Tansy said, nodding. Branch winked at her, and she gave him her lantern so that he could find his way in the dark.

"Would you mind sharing your lantern with me, ma'am?" she asked the woman. "Dropping a lantern in the grave wasn't supposed to be part of the tour."

Everyone chuckled, and the woman did indeed give her lantern to Tansy.

"It looks so real down there," one teenage boy said as he leaned over to peer into the grave again. "Seriously! That skeleton looks so real!"

Not wanting to comment that the skeleton looked so real because it *was* real, Tansy began walking toward another grave with a story behind it, in hopes that the crowd would really believe the Anouk grave was a setup and follow her.

"The story goes that Anouk's husband, Geert Van der Veen, wanted to preserve her beauty for as long as possible," she began. "So he contracted a porcelain coffin to be built for her at the time of her death. That a wooden coffin would've deteriorated much faster was his theory, and he hoped that the porcelain one would preserve her better."

"Why didn't he just have her embalmed?" the teenage girl holding tight to the teenage boy's hand inquired.

"Well, it was 1818, and embalming as we know it, at least, wasn't in practice yet," Tansy explained. Then motioning toward the receiving vault, she added, "On our way to the receiving vault, we'll pass the resting place of Danique Van der Veen, Geert Van der Veen's first wife. It was rumored, at the time of her death, that Geert had Danique murdered so that he could marry his mistress at the time, Anouk."

Although there were stragglers—those who just couldn't seem to tear their gazes away from what lay in Anouk Van der Veen's plundered grave—eventually every member of the tour party did manage to find their way to Danique Van der Veen's grave and then onto the receiving vault. Tansy was grateful that Mr. Brenden was in perfect Barnabas Collins form that night—for his appearance did seem to distract everyone from what they had seen at the Van der Veen gravesite. Yet as Tansy glanced over to see the golden light from the lantern beaming out of Anouk's grave, the eerie sight caused unpleasant goose bumps to riddle her arms. Who had done such a thing as to disturb the woman's final resting place? Even more disturbing was the fact that whoever had dug down to find Anouk's remains not only left the emerald jewels with her behind, proving that theft hadn't been the reason for the deed, but also morbidly plunged a wooden stake through her skeleton.

As Tansy listened to Mr. Brenden explaining the *Dark Shadows* history of the receiving vault to the mesmerized crowd, Tansy felt a shiver of ominous dread travel over her spine. Branch had literally saved her from falling directly into the open grave! What would've happened if he hadn't? She hated to think of the injuries she might have sustained. And although she prided herself on having a strong stomach, she hated to think of having fallen in the grave to find herself sprawled out with Anouk Van der Veen's remains even more!

Tansy scanned the darkness behind the crowd, hoping to see that Branch had returned. But he hadn't—not yet. So for the moment, Tansy rubbed the goose bumps from her arms and tried, in vain, to keep from looking back at the funnel of light rising from a grave that had not been disturbed for nearly two hundred years.

"So they didn't take the emeralds, hm?" Marvin asked.

Marvin was standing with Meredith and Mr. Brenden and several other of the cemetery tour volunteers.

"Nope," Meredith answered. "So obviously the intent wasn't theft."

Tansy shivered at the thought of the open grave. Certainly everyone, except the police, was behind the yellow crime scene tape, but somehow the whole intrusion on Anouk Van der Veen's grave seemed even worse now with the bright lights law enforcement had set up to illuminate the scene more clearly. Tansy also felt sad that Anouk's rumored, and obviously very real, porcelain casket had been shattered—the lid of it, anyway. But worst of all to Tansy's way of thinking was the stake someone had driven through her in the space where her heart had once been. Why would someone do such a thing?

"Maybe you better watch your back, Mr. Brenden," Marvin suggested, "being that someone is out to get vampires, it would seem."

"Not funny," Meredith scolded, frowning at Marvin.

"It's gruesome to say the least," Mr. Brenden said, ignoring Marvin's crass insensitivity.

Tansy shivered again.

"It is pretty cold out here tonight," Branch noted. "Here," he said, taking Tansy by the shoulders and moving her so that he stood directly behind her. "Maybe I can block the wind a little."

Block the wind a little? Tansy thought as the warmth of his body behind her began to radiate onto her back. *More like send me swooning!*

"Thanks," she said. "That actually helps a lot."

"I bet," Meredith whispered to her.

A police officer began striding away from the grave and toward the group of people they'd asked to wait nearby. Tansy and Branch had been interviewed first and then several of the tour group who had lingered after the tour. It seemed that Tansy hadn't managed to fool everyone in the group, for several of the guests had recognized the grave desecration was legitimate and thus had remained at the cemetery after the other guests had taken their leave just after midnight.

"Thank you for your help, everyone," the officer, whose nametag read *Van Tassel*, began. "We've got everything we need from each of you individuals. Why doesn't everyone just head home for now, all right?"

Everyone nodded, mumbled thank yous, and turned to leave.

Branch, however, reached out and shook the policeman's hand. "Thank you," he said. "And you have my information in case you need to ask me anything else, right?"

"We do," Officer Van Tassel said. "Thanks again."

"What will happen now?" Tansy couldn't help asking.

Officer Van Tassel exhaled a heavy sigh and then answered, "We'll start the process of finding out who did this." He shook his head with disgust. "Almost two hundred years, right? And then someone has to go and do this."

"Will…will the remains be reburied or something?" Tansy ventured.

"Oh, absolutely," Officer Van Tassel assured her. "I'm sure we'll have everything we need after tomorrow, and then whatever needs to be done to reinter the remains can begin."

Tansy exhaled a sigh of relief. "Oh, good," she said. "Thank you, officer."

Branch moved then, and Tansy felt a blast of cold air hit her back, sending another chill through her.

"You ready to go then?" he asked, shoving his hands into his pockets—for he wasn't wearing a jacket either.

"Yeah, I guess so," Tansy answered, "though I'm sure I'll never get to sleep tonight. I'm really kind of creeped out, you know?"

"I do," Branch affirmed. "I guess watching forensic shows on TV doesn't measure up to seeing real-life human remains."

"Amen to that!" Tansy giggled nervously.

"Well, let me at least walk you back to your car, okay?" Branch offered.

"Oh, thank you," Tansy said. Even after the morbid experience of finding Anouk Van der Veen's grave destroyed, Tansy's heart leapt at the idea that Branch was walking her to her car. She could still remember how it felt when he had saved her from falling into the open grave—how it felt when he had held her arm, his other arm around her waist. She loved thinking of the way he'd blocked the chilly autumn air from her back only moments before—how the heat from his body was like a warm heating pad against her back. She only wished she didn't have to leave him.

Suddenly she wondered—after all the drama the night had brought on them, would Branch still feel like taking her with him to tour the less-traveled haunts of Sleepy Hollow when morning came?

"Are you still up for taking me around town tomorrow, do you think?" Branch asked then.

Tansy gasped, looked at him with widened eyes, and said, "I was just this second wondering if *you* still wanted to go!"

Branch smiled. "Great minds think alike, they say, right?"

"They do say that," Tansy giggled.

"And I'm more up for it than ever...if you are, I mean," he ventured.

"Oh, me too!" she assured him. "I think it might be nice to steer clear of the cemetery for one day, as well."

"It would seem so," he agreed. He shook his head in disbelief as they headed toward the street where Tansy had parked. "The dude left the jewels. Weird, you know?"

"I know," Tansy agreed. "And what's with the stake through the heart? Poor Anouk."

"It really is a shame. Two hundred years she was there, undisturbed. And then some bast...some jerk does that," Branch said.

The unpleasant kind of goose bumps prickled Tansy's arms again as the foreboding, ominous sensation returned.

"I'm pretty sure it's going to take me awhile to get the image out of my head," Tansy remarked.

They had reached her car, and she pressed the fob on her keychain to unlock it.

"Thanks for walking me to my car," she said, turning and gazing up into the ultra, uber handsome face of her new favorite illustrator.

"Thanks for walking *me* to *my* car," he joked. Nodding to the space right behind her, Tansy looked to see his rental Dodge Charger, parked right behind her own car.

"Oh, how funny!" she laughed. Looking back to him, she said, "Do you still want to hit the road at nine in the morning? It's almost two now, so…"

"Aw, let's be lazy and make it ten, okay?" he asked.

Tansy nodded in expressing her agreement that they should meet later than they had planned. "Yeah, it'll probably take me three hours to drop off to sleep after all this, and I need a little shut-eye if I'm going to remember all the cool places I'd like you to see," she said.

"Good thinking," he chuckled. "You're sure you're okay to drive home this late by yourself and all? I mean, do you live alone?"

"I am, and I do." Tansy smiled at him. "And you're very kind to worry about me. But I rent one of my Dad's rental properties that is just around the corner from the orchard. So if I get too freaked out, I can run over to my parents' house. But I don't want you to think I'm a chicken. So let's just say that I'll make sure the doors and windows are locked and then turn on every light in my house before I go to bed, okay?"

Branch smiled and nodded. "All right…but I want to make sure you're okay."

"I really am fine," Tansy assured him. "No worries where I'm concerned. You just get a good night's sleep so your fingers will be all ready to sketch the wonders of Sleepy Hollow tomorrow." As a reflex, Tansy reached up and straightened the edge of Branch's shirt collar. "After all, you've got royalties to earn, right?"

"I do," Branch said as he reached out, brushing a stray strand of hair from Tansy's cheek.

This gesture caused fresh goose bumps—the blissful kind this time—to race over Tansy's arms and legs. She wondered for an instant how his hand could be so warm when it was so cold outside.

Tansy wasn't ready to say goodbye to Branch—even for the fact that it would only be a matter of hours before she saw him again. The realization struck her that she never, ever wanted to say goodbye to Branch—never.

Therefore, something deep in her that she couldn't control unexpectedly caused her to reach out and wrap her arms around his waist, hug him tightly, and say, "Thanks for not letting me tumble into that grave with Anouk's skeleton. I would've been traumatized for life…not to mention most likely cut to shreds on all that broken porcelain."

Knowing she'd been far too forward in hugging him, Tansy began to pull back from him.

Branch caught her face between his warm, strong hands, however, and she paused—for he was looking at her with dark green eyes—mesmerizing eyes that seemed to simmer with mischief, amusement, or something akin to desire. She couldn't be sure.

"We've known each other for what? Twenty-four hours now?" he asked, his voice low and hypnotically alluring.

"I-I suppose," Tansy managed to stammer in response.

"Well, I've never met anyone who intrigued and inspired me more in the course of twenty-four hours than you have, Tansy," Branch said. "My mind is so packed with ideas for art that I can't even sift them into categories yet—and that's from just the few times we've spoken, you know?"

"Really?" Tansy asked, blushing with delight. She'd never thought, in all her wildest dreams, that she'd be inspiration for art somehow. Even though she knew it wasn't really art of herself she'd inspired—even though she knew that Sleepy Hollow, New York, just had a way of drawing in everyone who ever visited—she was flattered that Branch would think it was her that inspired him.

"And that makes me wonder," he almost mumbled, "how much more you might inspire me if I were to…"

Tansy held her breath, too stunned by the fact that Branch's head was descending toward hers to worry about breathing. He was going to kiss her! He really was! After only having just met him the day before—the night before—he was brazen enough to try and kiss her. The even crazier thing was that Tansy *wanted* him to kiss her! She'd actually wanted him to kiss her from the very moment the night before when she'd looked out and seen him in the tour group— though it was such a scandalous thought that she never would've confessed it to anyone.

Yet now, as Branch's head descended—as Tansy felt the first touch of his lips to hers—as every cell in her body felt as if it had just been sent to an euphoric boiling point—Tansy sighed with a sort of effervescent intoxication.

Branch's hands were warm against her face, and she could feel the calluses on his palms. Being suddenly hyper-aware of every sensation of him, she wondered briefly how his hands managed to be callused like a farmer's when he was, in fact, an artist.

But even that contemplation was lost to Tansy as Branch's initially tentative kiss grew more intense. Tansy felt her hands at his waist begin to fist the fabric of his shirt in her hands—for his kiss, almost careful and uncertain, was literally causing her toes to clench in her shoes. She wanted to wrap her arms around his neck, pull herself tight against him, and kiss him like she hoped he'd never been kissed before! Instead, she bridled her desire to kiss him more intimately and instead bathed in and returned the moist, careful kisses Branch was orchestrating between them. After all, they had only known each other twenty-four hours. Tansy didn't want Branch to think she was a hoochie.

Branch's hands were literally numb with the spectacular effect Tansy's kiss was rinsing through him. He'd kissed girls before—even after only one date. But nothing had ever affected him the way kissing Tansy was affecting him! He felt as if he were on the verge of losing control—of lifting her into his arms and just going for it. In addition to the staggering physical effects kissing her was having on him (and they weren't even kissing intensely), the images flashing through his mind as he kissed her were near overwhelming—color, texture, light, and shadow. The thought flashed in Branch's mind, *Is this what it's like when an artist finds his muse?* He had never been so bombarded with inspiration, and he knew it was Tansy's doing.

Branch found his self-control was quickly weakening. So with one final, pretty darn driven kiss, he unwillingly pulled back from her. Still holding her face between his hands, Branch grinned at her as he studied her pretty, pretty, pretty face.

"Too much?" he asked as he began to worry that he'd been too forward.

He grinned, however, when Tansy shook her head, smiled at him, and said, "Not at all. After all, you did save my life earlier…so I owed you a big thank you, you know?"

Branch's smile broadened with relief—and a little bit of masculine pride in the fact he hadn't grossed her out.

"So I'll see you at ten in the morning?" he asked.

"See you at ten," Tansy said.

Branch opened her car door for her then, closing it once she'd settled into the driver's seat.

"Good night," he said as she waved at him through the window.

Tansy started her car and then drove off, tossing him a cute little wave as she did.

Branch exhaled a heavy breath of satisfaction. Tansy was awesome! And kissing her had been phenomenal. He watched her car disappear around a corner before he got into his own car.

As he drove back to his hotel, Branch couldn't keep ideas for both books he was illustrating from ricocheting around in his head like a wad of Flubber. Furthermore, he was pretty awed by the fact that his mind was so full of ideas—that it seemed he'd found his muse. For one thing, he'd never believed there was such a thing— one woman who could singularly and entirely inspire an artist. It had all seemed like the Greek and Roman mythology concerning Zeus's nine daughters, the muses—goddesses of the inspiration of art, literature, and science. Yep, Branch had always thought that the idea of an artist having a muse was just that—mythology.

Yet from the moment he'd first seen Tansy the night before—all dressed up like a revolutionary Van Tassel—his mind had begun to bulge with ideas for new work—illustrations, paintings, novels. At first he'd attributed it to the fact that Sleepy Hollow was teaming with atmosphere. Yet by the end of his first Sleepy Hollow cemetery tour, he'd known it was more than that—that it was Tansy. And when that very morning she'd appeared while he'd been sketching the cemetery fence, the same thing had happened—near overwhelming inspiration! Then again at her family's orchard. And that very night during his second, and very eventful, cemetery tour. But the final icing on the cake—Branch's final assurance that Tansy Sheridan was destined to be his muse—was the kiss they'd shared. His mind and body had never felt so alive as when he'd kissed her. Furthermore, Branch figured that all of it together—the way Tansy inspired him, the way he felt when he was with her, and the fact that he could not get her out of his mind even for a moment—all of it was causing him to think that the girl was destined to be far more than his muse. Twenty-four hours—maybe twenty-seven or twenty-eight—and Branch Jackman, who was normally very practical and logical in his thinking, was wondering what kind of engagement ring the girl would prefer.

Shaking his head to try and dispel such teenager-in-love type thoughts, Branch tuned the satellite radio to the Classic Rock station. Maybe a little loud rock-and-roll would help him straighten out his ludicrous musings where his newfound muse was concerned.

♥

Evening's crisp and cooler now.
The frantic harvest eases.
The leaves of orange and gold and brown
Swirl past with October breezes.

Exhaling a heavy sigh of contentment, Tansy closed her book—her copy of *October Breezes*—*October Breezes*, written by Windy Lyrant and illustrated by Branch Jackman. She studied the cover for a moment. It was incredible to think that Branch had illustrated the book—and not just any book but the very book that Tansy had framed pages from to adorn the small hallway of her house.

She ran her hand over the beautiful cover illustration, imagining that somehow doing so would connect her to Branch. She couldn't wait until morning—couldn't wait to see him again—couldn't wait to spend the day with him!

Laying the book to one side, Tansy turned off the lamp on her nightstand. It was, in truth, the only light in the house that was actually turned off, for she was sure that the memory of discovering Anouk Van der Veen's vandalized grave was still too fresh in her mind to sleep comfortably in the dark.

Tansy was pleased when she closed her eyes to find that, instead of lingering visions of poor Anouk's skeleton, it was the image of Branch that met her. In fact, her thoughts of Branch—of his masterful kiss—caused such a warm, delicious pleasantness to fill her body that Tansy felt herself begin to drift to sleep much more quickly than she would've thought she'd be able to.

"Branch Jackman," Tansy whispered aloud to herself. "I love your name."

Thus, with Branch's name on her lips—with the sensational memory of his kiss there as well—with images of his enchanting illustrations for *October Breezes* and his handsome face filling her mind—Tansy Sheridan was soon fast asleep.

CHAPTER FIVE

"Yeah, everyone at the hotel was talking about it this morning," Branch explained as he drove back toward town.

Branch had arrived at the orchard promptly at ten a.m. to pick her up. She still could hardly believe she was sitting in the passenger's seat of his rental car, on her way to spend the day with him. But as she glanced over at him as he was telling her how abuzz the hotel staff was that morning, she was reassured that she was awake and with him—not just dreaming.

When Branch had first arrived to collect her, Tansy hadn't been sure she could look him in the eye without blushing. After all, the kiss they'd shared the night before was quite—well, it wasn't the kind of kiss people shared when they'd only known each other one day—at least not to Tansy's way of thinking and experience.

Still, Branch had seemed so calm and comfortable when he'd arrived that morning to begin their day together that her worries about being bashful in his presence evaporated pretty quickly. Furthermore, he looked so handsome, dressed in his flannel shirt, jeans, and worn work boots, that Tansy was determined to capture and keep his interest.

"I mean, why didn't whoever dug up the grave take the jewels, you know?" Branch asked. "The cops say they're the real deal, so it makes no sense."

"And the stake through the heart thing was weird," Tansy added. She wrinkled her nose a moment as an odd thought struck her. "Maybe Mr. Brenden has lost his marbles and thinks he really is Barnabas Collins or something. Of course, vampires don't usually stake other vampires, right? Meaning that if he thought Anouk Van der Veen was…"

She glanced over to see Branch grinning at her with an expression of pleased amusement.

Blushing a little, Tansy shook her head and said, "Sorry. Sometimes my imagination can be a little ridiculous."

But Branch simply responded, "Well, I actually wondered the same thing."

"So you don't think I'm nuts?" Tansy giggled.

"Not at all," Branch assured her. "I'm sure the thought crossed the cops' minds too."

"Probably," Tansy agreed. She was quiet for a moment and then commented, "Well, I hope that's not it. I'd hate to think Mr. Brenden was a whack job."

"The whole thing doesn't seem quite as creepy in the light of day anyway," Branch offered.

"Nope. Though, to be honest, I'm kind of curious and would like to take a look into that grave when it's light outside and I'm not so startled. It's a once-in-a-lifetime opportunity and would be so interesting, really," Tansy suggested.

"Me too," Branch said. "But the cops still have it all roped off and guarded." He glanced to her and smiled, adding, "I checked this morning before I came to pick you up."

Tansy laughed. "Well, you know what they say about great minds."

"Exactly," Branch chuckled. "I did stay up sketching last night when I got back to my room though. I couldn't settle down. There was just too much going through my mind."

"Oh no!" Tansy exclaimed. "How long did you stay up?"

Branch just shrugged and answered, "I don't know. I went to sleep while it was still dark, so it couldn't have been that late."

"Are you sure you're up for this today?" Tansy asked. "I mean, if you're too tired, we can reschedule."

Again Branch glanced at her, grinning. "Do I look too tired?"

Tansy smiled. "No. Not at all, actually." He didn't look tired. He looked wide awake and gorgeous!

"Yep. I'm wide awake and raring to go!"

Rubbing her hands together with excitement, Tansy said, "Okay! Then let's start with the bridge."

"The bridge?" Branch asked.

"Yeah. You probably have already seen it, probably even walked over it, since a lot of people like to believe it's the old bridge that actually was in the Sleepy Hollow cemetery. But the original is long gone—although our local historians have documented at least five places where bridges where the Albany Post Road once crossed the Pocantico River in, like, the late 1700s. And even though the rustic-looking bridge in the Sleepy Hollow cemetery is the best one for tourist photo ops, I have my favorite elsewhere, and I like to believe that *it's* the one that Washington Irving was thinking of when he wrote 'The Legend of Sleepy Hollow.' So…do you wanna see that first?"

"Sounds like a great place to start," Branch agreed. "Just tell me where to turn and stuff, okay?"

"Of course," Tansy assured him. "And you'll love it! It's a beautiful place!"

"No doubt," Branch said. "Especially being that everything around here is beautiful."

Tansy blushed with delight as he looked at her, winking with a silent implication that she was one of the beautiful everythings around there. Tansy felt her toes curl inside her shoes—she was that delighted by his flirting.

♥

"I take it that you're inspired?" Tansy said.

Branch grinned as he looked up to the incredible autumn vista before him. Sketching as quickly as he could—for he didn't want to waste too much of his day with Tansy on work—he answered, "Very."

"It is beautiful out here, isn't it?" Tansy asked. "I love that they built this bridge to look old and rickety. It's only been here a few years, but it looks like it's been here a hundred."

Branch nodded as he added some more shadow to his sketch. "You guys have incredible falls too," he remarked. "I mean, I've been east this time of year before, but this place is awesome! I'm sure the seclusion helps too. You know, it's not all trampled up by tourists."

"That's one reason I love it so much," Tansy explained. "It's very isolated, and most of the locals…well, they're pretty busy with life, you know? I think people start to lose their appreciation for a place when they live their everyday life surrounded by it…if they're not careful, that is." Tansy sighed with satisfaction—for the area was thriving with trees, grass, moss-covered rocks, and of course the lovely stream running under the bridge.

A breeze suddenly wafted through the trees, sending red and orange leaves swirling everywhere, and Tansy smiled, for it looked exactly as if a group of invisible pixies were twirling along, kicking leaves up as they went.

"It's why I try to focus on how lucky I am to live here," she added. "I try really hard to appreciate the beauty of my surroundings every day. It takes some forethought actually. With work and stuff, it's hard to remember to stop and smell the roses, you know?"

"Or to stop and smell the horse manure, as my grandpa would always say," Branch added, smiling.

Tansy was quiet for a few moments and then asked, "Does it bother you if I talk? If I'm talking too much, please let me know."

Branch's grin broadened into a smile. She was adorable! And he loved the sound of her voice. Usually he had trouble focusing on his work when someone was talking to him. But with Tansy—well, it was like he was able to draw more quickly—conjure up images in an instant that usually took him minutes or hours to conjure.

"Not at all," he told her. Pausing, he put his pad and pencil down, leaned back on his hands where he sat, crossed his feet at his ankles, and looked at her. "I wasn't kidding when I told you last night that you inspire me."

Tansy's eyes widened with obvious astonishment. "What? What're you talking about?"

"Last night," Branch reiterated. "When I told you that you inspire me, that I think you're my muse—although I never thought artists really had muses...until I met you, of course."

"Y-you think I'm your muse?" she asked, her eyes sparkling like starlight.

"Yeah," Branch said. "I told you that last night." He frowned a moment, trying to remember their conversation of the night before, just before Tansy drove away in her car. "At least, I thought I told you that." Again he thought back. Then he chuckled and smiled, explaining, "Oh, wait, I didn't tell you. I kissed you instead. I guess I thought you could read my mind or something."

Tansy was quiet for a while—quiet as she stared at Branch in obvious disbelief. Finally, she said, "Well, that's either the most wonderful thing anyone has ever told me...or the best pickup line in the world!" Smiling at him with an expression of amused doubt, she asked, "But you're kidding, right?"

Branch shook his head. "Nope. I'm as serious as the business end of a .45."

Tansy smiled, amused by Branch's idiom. "Where are you from?" she asked then. "I mean, you've never told me where you're from. But a couple of things you've said leads me to believe you're from...well, if not from the south, from somewhere with personality."

Branch chuckled as he sketched. "I'm from Texas. Is it that obvious?"

Tansy giggled—for she was, for some reason, wildly pleased by the fact that Branch was from Texas.

"No, not really," she answered. "It was just your reference to horse manure and then a .45. I figured you were from somewhere interesting."

"Abilene, Texas, actually. And it is someplace interesting...at least to me," Branch added.

Tansy studied him from head to toe for a minute or two. "Hmmm. But no Wranglers? No cowboy boots?" she prodded.

Again Branch chuckled. "Not here," he answered. "Not when I'm trying to fit in to the local scene, you know? If there's one thing I don't like, it's standing out in a crowd, you know? I like to blend in, remain unnoticed as much as possible."

"Because of your work?" Tansy asked, although she simultaneously thought that there was no way Branch could ever blend in to a crowd and remain unnoticed—not with his hotness!

Branch shrugged. "Yeah, I guess. But mostly I just don't like being the center of attention, you know? It makes me uncomfortable and self-conscious."

"But when you're home? How about then? Wranglers and cowboy boots?" Tansy inquired, and she was sincerely interested. She figured there was no way Branch could be any better looking than he already was, but as she imagined him dressed in worn western wear, she felt goose bumps prickling her arms.

"Levi's and boots," Branch said, looking up from his sketchpad and winking at her.

"Yet you're an artist? An illustrator and graphic novelist? I thought maybe you'd be…I don't know, like a farm boy or something," Tansy offered.

"Farm *boy*?" Branch asked, feigning indignity and offense at her suggesting he was only a boy.

Tansy laughed. "Okay, farm *man* then."

"Damn right, farm man," Branch mumbled, grinning as he returned his attention to his sketching. Shrugging, he added, "Oh, I buck bales, ride horses, and herd cattle with the best of them when I'm home helping my dad out. But it's almost impossible to make a good living at that anymore. So since I always liked drawing, even as a kid…" He shrugged again, explaining, "Well, I kind of fell into it in a way…and I just kept going."

"Kind of like me and apples," Tansy commented. "I mean, there's not a whole lot of money in apples anymore either. So that's why I work on preserving different varieties and things like that." She glanced across the stream to the trees and vines Branch was sketching. "Did you know that before industrial agriculture hit the world, there were thousands of different varieties of apples grown in the U.S. alone? But now there are only about five or six varieties grown for the grocery industry. So when I was a little girl, Daddy and I quartered off a section in one of our older orchards where we'd taken out some trees and began planting heirloom trees…or varieties that were nearly extinct. It's kind of my pet project." She shrugged. "But we are finding that more and more people are requesting grafts from some of our trees to start heirloom orchards of their own. So that makes us feel good about doing it. My dream is to get ahold of a Harrison apple graft someday."

Again Branch paused in sketching and looked at her. "A Harrison apple? Is it rare?"

Tansy nodded. "Oh, very! In the early 1800s, it was renowned for the cider it produced—touted as the finest in the world, actually. But in 1976, a guy found one tree at an old abandoned cider mill in Livingston, New Jersey. He grafted it, and Harrison apple trees are now beginning to bear fruit again. I'd love to have a Harrison apple tree one day. Mmm!"

Tansy turned to see Branch staring at her with a dazzling smile of approval on his handsome face. "So that's your passion: apples," he stated.

"I guess so," she said. "Although I never quite thought of it that way…as my passion. And I guess yours is art, huh?"

Tansy was surprised, however, when Branch actually shook his head and said, "Nope. Art is my job…and I guess a hobby of sorts."

Tansy frowned. "Really? Then what's your passion?"

"Well, before I met you—horses," he said.

"Before you met me?" Tansy asked as her heart began to race. "Wh-what do you mean by that?"

"I mean exactly what I said…that before I met you, horses were my passion. But now, I think my muse—that's you—is going to be my passion, and horses will be my secondary interest," he answered.

Tansy stared at him in disbelief. Was he kidding? Surely he was kidding! But he wasn't laughing or even smiling, really. He was simply looking up at the trees across the stream, then down to his sketchpad as he sketched, and back to the trees.

"Wow!" Tansy said, at last. "You *are* good! Did you take lessons on how to charm women or what?"

"Not at all," he answered. "You just asked me what my passion was, and I told you."

Tansy continued to stare at Branch—continued to watch him look down as he sketched, then glance up at their surroundings, and then look down as he sketched again. He appeared to be completely sincere.

Unexpectedly then, Branch began to laugh a bit as he sketched. Figuring that he'd finally broken and was no longer able to keep a straight face about Tansy's being his muse and passion, she actually felt an incredibly powerful wave of disappointment wash over her. She liked Branch so, so, so very much—liked him more with every moment she spent in his company. She couldn't explain to herself why; it was just a fact. Therefore, his teasing her about being his passion was more painful than flattering.

"I gotta tell you something," Branch began. "Last night…and I'm not making light of the grave thing, you know? I mean, it was terrible, that someone dug up that lady's grave and did what they did.

But I have to admit that as we were walking away from it, I looked back…and you know how the lantern light was shining up out of the grave?"

"Y-yeah," Tansy agreed, uncertain as to what his point was—and now completely confused about whether he'd been kidding her about her being his muse.

"Well, it reminded me of this time that I went to summer camp when I was thirteen," Branch continued. "My mom had bought me this new flashlight…like, this really high-end looking flashlight, you know?"

"Uh huh," Tansy prodded, her mind still trying to sort out everything Branch had said before and then how he could possibly go from telling her she was his passion to talking about some flashlight he took to camp when he was thirteen.

"I knew things were tight for Mom and Dad…you know, financially," Branch continued. "So I was kind of upset that my mom had purchased such an expensive flashlight for me to take to camp. After all, everyone knows that anything you hand to a thirteen-year-old boy, especially when he's going to be camping, is going to get lost or destroyed, right?"

"Right," Tansy confirmed—although she knew nothing about thirteen-year-old boys going to summer camp.

"So I was uptight about this flashlight the whole time I was at camp…which I hated, by the way," Branch explained. "And then, one night, I had to go." He paused, glanced to Tansy, and said, "You know…go…to the bathroom."

"Oh…oh! I see," Tansy said, realizing what Branch was trying to convey.

"Anyway," he continued, even as he kept sketching, "I grabbed the snazzy flashlight Mom had given me and headed toward the latrines." He paused, shaking his head. "I'd rather go outside *anywhere* than have to use those grodie latrines at the campsites. Anyway, as I was…preparing to do my business, I accidentally dropped my brand-new, high-powered flashlight down into the sludge beneath the latrine seat." He chuckled, sighed, and shook his head again—all the time still sketching the beautiful landscape before him. "I was freaked out. I was sure my mom had paid a hundred bucks for that stupid flashlight, but there wasn't any way I was going to try to fish it out."

Tansy frowned, confused by the fact that the disturbing grave robbery they'd discovered the night before had somehow sparked the flashlight at summer camp memory for Branch.

"I don't get it," she admitted. "What does that have to do with the grave desecration at the cemetery?"

Branch grinned. "Well, last night, when we walked away and I looked back to see that lantern light beaming up out of that grave, it reminded me of the flashlight thing. You see, when I dropped the flashlight down the latrine hole, it was still turned on. I'd used it to find my way from my tent to the latrine. As fate would have it, it landed in the sludge pointing directly up. So for the next two nights, there was this radiant beam of white light beaming up out of the roofless top of the latrine and into the night sky. It looked like one of those search lights they use to advertise stuff."

Branch chuckled to himself again. "It was pretty funny because you know how guys are. All the scouts would try to douse the flashlight light by hitting it when they…you know…used the latrine to…to rid themselves of their solid waste. You know what I mean?"

Tansy giggled—more at being amused at how delicately Branch tried to refer to human feces than by the flashlight light beaming out into the night sky.

Branch shook his head, still amused by the memory. "That was some flashlight, or some batteries Mom had put in it, because it was a beacon for that latrine for over forty-eight hours."

"And when you got home, was your mom upset that you'd lost the flashlight?" Tansy asked. She hated to think of little Branch Jackman getting chewed out over losing a flashlight down the latrine—hated to think that it may have been a financial burden on his parents just to provide the flashlight.

"No, not at all," Branch answered. "Of course, I did nothing but worry about it the whole rest of the week at camp. You know, worried that I'd lost something my parents had had to sacrifice to provide for me. But when I got home and told my mom, she told me that the flashlight only cost $6.95. You know, she told me that as she was laughing so hard about the illuminated latrine story that I thought she was going to rupture something."

Tansy smiled, glad that Branch hadn't gotten in trouble for dropping his flashlight down the latrine hole.

"Yeah, it's a whole family thing now," Branch added. "I swear, my mom still can't pick up a flashlight without at least grinning a little. But it was traumatizing for me."

Unexpectedly then, Branch closed his sketchbook, tossed it and his pencil into the grass at his side, and drew his knees up to lean on them as he looked at Tansy. "So that's what the light coming out of the grave last night reminded me of. Random…I know."

"I like that you told me that," Tansy admitted. "It actually reveals a lot about you—your concern for your parents, your sense of humor, and your ability to be amused by even something as creepy as that whole grave thing last night."

"Maybe," Branch said. "But mostly it just shows what a worry-wart-ish idiot I was as an awkward teen…barely a teen at that."

"Oh, I have a really hard time believing you were ever awkward…teenager or not," Tansy said.

"Why?" he asked, and the question caught Tansy majorly off guard.

"W-well…because," she stammered in response. She could feel her cheeks beginning to blush with the heat of embarrassment.

"Because why?" Branch prodded.

Tansy caught the hint of mischief in his eyes and figured he liked making her uncomfortable.

"Well, b-because you're so…so accomplished and everything now," she managed to sputter.

"Accomplished?" Branch asked, smiling with doubt. "A concert pianist is accomplished. I'm just a gun-toting farm boy from Texas who draws stuff. Or did you forget that part?"

"Everything you listed is an accomplishment," Tansy reminded him. "It's not like you're an apple-picking cemetery tour guide, you know?"

"An heirloom-apple-growing, cemetery historian," Branch playfully argued.

Tansy felt her brows pucker with curiosity. "Gun-toting farm boy? Really?"

Branch nodded emphatically and stated, "Absolutely and always…as long as whatever state I'm in recognizes my concealed carry permit. Of course, I had to apply for a permit to carry here long before I arrived. I'm just glad my permit came through in time."

Tansy smiled. "Well, well, aren't you just Mr. Plan Ahead."

Branch laughed. "Yeah, I guess I am."

"We should go shooting sometime," Tansy suggested.

She smiled with feeling proud when Branch's eyebrows arched in surprise. "You shoot?"

"I do," Tansy confirmed. "And I have my concealed carry permit too. Although, unlike you, I don't carry all the time."

Branch's eyes narrowed, seeming to simmer with approval or something like it as he studied her face a moment.

"Well, you just get more and more delicious, don't you, Tansy Sheridan," he said in a lowered, pretty darn provocative voice.

Tansy blushed from her head to her pinky toes. "Oh, I don't know about that," she bashfully mumbled.

"Well, I do…so trust me," he said.

Exhaling an almost heavy sigh, Branch rose to his feet and offered a hand to Tansy to help her stand.

She took his hand, of course, and was instantly awash with a warm, delightful sensation that began in her palm and radiated up her arm. Branch pulled her to her feet, and Tansy brushed off the seat of her jeans.

"Where to now?" he asked.

Tansy shrugged. "What are you in the mood for? More bridges? More trees? Houses? People?"

"Whatever you think," Branch said. "And if you want to grab some lunch first, we can do that. I'm kind of hungry. Do you know a good place in town, or not too far from where we are?"

"Oh, I do!" Tansy exclaimed. "My favorite, favorite little place is right on our way to some of the old houses I thought you might like to see. It's called the Horseman's Tavern, and it is *so* yummy! You'll love it!"

"Let's hit that then before we do anything else, okay?" Branch agreed.

Tansy smiled and turned to head back to where they'd parked a ways down the road. But she stopped when Branch reached out and caught her hand.

"I…um…I did want to ask you if you were ticked off at me for kissing you last night," he said. "I don't want you thinking I'm a player or anything like that. And I'm not some freak psycho either. I just really, really, really do like you, Tansy."

Tansy felt the warmth rise to her cheeks—thought she might burst into spouting butterflies from her ears, she was so pleased with what Branch was telling her.

"Well, at the risk of sounding like a coo-coo myself…I really, really, really like you too, Branch," she admitted.

Branch grinned as he slowly pulled Tansy toward him and into his arms.

"It's kind of weird, huh?" he asked as she gazed up into his deep green eyes. "I've known you, what? Forty hours or something like that? Not even two days. And yet I feel like I've known you all my life." He winked at her and smiled, adding, "And that's not a pickup line, by the way."

Tansy giggled. "I'm glad," she said, "'cause I feel the same way. It kind of freaks me out because…I mean, aren't you supposed to know someone a way long time before you…before you like them so much?"

Branch shrugged. "I always thought so. But who knows? Anything is possible, I guess."

Tansy had to ask him then. She had to know if he was just teasing her—playing games with her—or if he meant what he'd said about her being his muse.

"Do you really mean that…what you said about me being your muse?" she ventured. "Or were you just feeding me a—"

"I really meant it," Branch assured her. "I swear, I have so many ideas banging around in my head it's giving me a headache." Tansy smiled as he added, "That…and I'm hungrier than I wanted to admit to you."

"But it doesn't make any sense that I would, you know, give you ideas," she explained.

Branch shook his head. "Yeah, well, I've learned that not everything makes sense. In fact, I think less stuff makes sense than does makes sense…if that makes sense."

Tansy smiled and allowed her arms to encircle Branch's waist. Branch. It truly did seem like she'd known him before—or forever. It was an odd feeling—the impression she was having that if he asked her to marry him then and there, she'd say yes and never even doubt it. There was no logic to it whatsoever, and yet it was the way she felt.

"I'm glad you don't think I'm crazy for confessing to you that I like you so much already," Branch mumbled.

Tansy felt his hands slip around her neck—felt his fingers in her hair—felt him fist her hair in his hands.

Damn, she was beautiful! Her eyes were the exact color of melted milk chocolate. And her lips were such a perfect pink that, if he hadn't known better, he would've sworn they'd been painted on her face by some master artist—an artist much more skilled than he was.

Branch wanted to kiss Tansy again—kiss her more thoroughly than he had the night before. But he didn't want to freak her out— make her doubt the sincerity of what he'd told her about the way he was feeling about her.

He paused for a moment, studying her face. Maybe he really had lost his mind. How could he possibly feel so strongly about a girl he'd known less than two days? But the fact was that he did! Every part of him was drawn to her like a moth to a bug zapper. It was as if, when he gazed into Tansy's eyes, he could see his future—his whole life from that moment on stretched out before him, beckoning him to jump in and live life with Tansy—and that doing so would be an everlasting happiness he'd never imagined.

A breeze blew several strands of Tansy's hair across her pretty face, and as she gazed up at him—gazed up at him the way no woman had ever gazed up at him before—Branch said, "I'm going to do it again, you know."

"What do you think I'm standing here waiting for?" Tansy asked in a whisper.

Without another instant's hesitation, Branch drew Tansy's face to his and kissed her firm and square on the mouth. More than that, he didn't feel like Mickey Mousing around either—and so he didn't.

Branch exhaled a sigh of satisfaction when he felt Tansy melt against him, pulling herself tight against his body. She felt small and fragile in his arms, and he worried for a moment that he might break her as he wrapped her in tensed arms to communicate the feeling of possessing her he was experiencing as he deepened the intensity of their kiss.

Tansy was in heaven! She didn't even care that the five-o'clock shadow Branch boasted when it wasn't even noon yet chafed the tender flesh of her lips and around her mouth. Almost instantly she was aware that there was a mutual sort of rhythm to the way Branch kissed her and she kissed him. His mouth was warm, moist, and somehow so familiar, and Tansy found herself dizzy from the near consuming sense that her soul or her heart or some deep part of her had known Branch her whole life.

Over and over he kissed her! And each kiss they shared seemed to grow with intensity. Tansy had never been so overwhelmed with attraction—desire—and it frightened her a little. But each time her mind would begin to whisper—*You've only known him two days!*—her heart would holler, *He's your soul mate! Do not ever let him go!*

Branch chuckled and, much to Tansy's disappointment, broke the seal of their lips when his stomach growled as if he hadn't eaten in a month.

"Sorry," he mumbled, shaking his head with obvious humiliation. "If I don't eat every two hours, my body thinks it's going to shrivel up and die."

Tansy giggled. After all, it was cute—the fact that Branch's stomach growling had interrupted their fantastically affecting exchange.

"I'm sorry I kept you so long out here," she said as he released her, stooping to pick up his sketchpad and pencil.

"It's not your fault I'm a caveman and have to eat an entire cow to feel full," Branch said.

Smiling at Tansy, he placed his large, muscular left arm across her shoulders, tucking her neatly against him and kissing her on the top of the head. Instinctively, Tansy put her arm around his waist, slipping her hand into the right back pocket of his jeans. She was momentarily awed into silence at how natural it seemed for her to do that—as if she'd been doing it for years.

"Okay then," she said. "Off to the Horseman's Tavern for a side of beef before we head out to see some of the older architecture around this place, okay?"

"Sounds great," Branch agreed as they began walking back toward the car.

Who would've guessed that precious little Tansy Sheridan was so easy? After all, how long had she known the guy—a day?

Marvin shook his head as he stepped out from behind several large trees where he'd stood watching Tansy and the tourist guy. He wondered if Meredith knew that her friend was already macking with some guy she'd met at the cemetery tour. Marvin figured that if Meredith didn't know, then somebody ought to tell her. And why not him?

When he'd gone out to the old bridge to pick up some acorns at his mom's request for some stupid craft thing she was working on, Marvin had never guessed he'd stumble across Tansy Sheridan and some stranger acting like they'd known each other all their lives.

Smiling, and with a plastic grocery sack full of acorns clutched in his hands, Marvin hurried toward his mom's house just around the bend from the bridge. He couldn't wait to tell Meredith about Tansy. Because if there was one thing Meredith liked, it was a bit of first-class gossip—and boy, oh, boy, did Marvin have the goods now!

CHAPTER SIX

The entire day had been nothing less than incredible. Of course, Tansy reasoned that any day spent in the company of Branch would be incredible, but this day—wow! After Branch had kissed her just before leaving the stream bank by the bridge, Tansy found she was so comfortable in Branch's company, every one of her lingering nervous jitters had simply evaporated.

They'd enjoyed lunch at the Horseman's Tavern together— lingered so long after finishing their meal that Branch tipped the waitress generously to compensate for any other tips she might've missed during the three hours they'd spent in the booth. And during all that time—which seemed to fly by to Tansy—never once did the conversation become awkward or die down. It was truly the most incredible lunch Tansy had ever experienced in all her life! They'd been at the restaurant so long, in fact, Branch had to stop in at the bakery next door to the Horseman's Tavern to grab a quick snack before they ventured out to see some of the historic homes Tansy had in mind. It was proof that Branch hadn't been exaggerating when he'd claimed he had to eat every two hours—and Tansy thought it very endearing.

Tansy was pleased at how many times Branch would hunker down in front of an old building or even sit right down on the sidewalk to begin sketching some of the historic architecture her hometown had to offer. They walked around Sleepy Hollow for quite some time, talking, laughing, learning more and more about one another—and of course, pausing so Branch could sketch. But even for all the time they'd had together that day, Tansy felt anxiety begin to rise in her as the sun began to set. Her beautiful day with Branch was almost over! All too soon she'd be back in her own house with nothing to think about but Branch, nothing to do but long for his company—and his kiss.

"Wow," Branch said as they walked back toward the center of town where he'd parked. "The temperature is really dropping."

Tansy had noticed how chilly it had gotten as well. The light sweatshirt she'd brought with her was hardly doing anything to warm her. But she wasn't about to complain or even show the littlest sign of how cold she really was. She didn't want Branch to think she was a whiner, and she certainly didn't want him to cut their day short for the sake that she was cold.

So she simply commented, "Yep. That's how it is this time of year. It'll just get colder and colder and colder. Then, before you know it, it will be Halloween, then Thanksgiving, and then Christmas. And with New Year's Eve, all the fun will be over for, like, four or five whole months."

Branch chuckled. "I take it you're not a fan of winter?"

"Well, in moderation," Tansy began to explain. "But it wears on me after a while, you know?"

"I do know," Branch agreed with a nod. "We do have winter in Texas, believe it or not. But nothing like out here."

"Yeah, it gets pretty cold sometimes," Tansy remarked as her anxiety knowing she would have to part from him soon began to grow.

"Is there anywhere close where we can get some dinner?" Branch asked.

"Dinner?" Tansy giggled. "You're hungry again?"

Branch shrugged. "Yeah...kind of. I mean, if you're not hungry, maybe you'd be willing to come with me and have some, I don't know, hot chocolate or warm cider or something like that. And I could just down a burger real quick."

Tansy's darkening mood brightened at his suggestion that they have dinner together.

"I'd love that!" she admitted, wondering afterward whether she'd seemed a little too eager.

"Great! Then point me in the right direction, and let's go," Branch said.

Tansy smiled—felt warmth drizzle over every inch of her body as he again put a muscular arm around her shoulders. She loved his touch in itself, but when he put his arm around her like this, it seemed so possessive that it just thrilled her to the very marrow of her bones!

"Let's go to Hathcock's," she said. "It's a cute little place with great burgers *and* hot chocolate."

"Sounds perfect," Branch agreed.

Placing her arm around his waist, Tansy slipped her hand into Branch's right back pocket and nodded to Hathcock's, which was not too far ahead of them up the street. She wasn't hungry at all, of course, but she was sure glad that every two hours Branch was.

♥

As six o'clock rolled around, Tansy was sitting across a booth table in Hathcock's staring at Branch as he downed a bacon cheeseburger, fries, and a milkshake. She was on her second mug of hot chocolate, which had easily satisfied any tiny twinges of hunger she might have had, and she was mesmerized in watching Branch—in hanging on every word he said.

"So I told her why I was here—to work on a graphic novel of Sleepy Hollow and illustrate a children's book—and she led me straight back to the archives," Branch was explaining. "You should see the information, microfiche, photographs, and records they've got in there. It's awesome! I could spend a decade in there and still not get through it all."

"Wow! You must've really charmed Mrs. Sturbridge," Tansy noted. "She's not normally so willing to let strangers set a finger on anything the historical society has in the private sector, let alone look through it unattended for hours."

And it was true! Tansy knew Mrs. Sturbridge well. The woman had been one of her history teachers in high school, and Tansy had dreaded her class every single day of her freshman year.

Branch smiled. "I sort of picked up on that right away, so I just flattered the hell out of her, and she gave me exactly what I needed," he explained.

"So then," Tansy began, suddenly curious, "how long were you in town before you attended your first cemetery tour?"

"Four days," he answered. "I like to do all kinds of research—you know, get to know the history of a place, kind of sit around and spy on the residents, stuff like that. Then when someone at the hotel told me you guys had a cemetery tour…well, I've always loved stuff like that, so I decided to go to one." He looked up from the hamburger he was holding, winked at her, and added, "And I'm so glad I did. Otherwise, I might have gone my whole life without finding my muse, right?"

Tansy shook her head as a breathy laugh escaped her throat. "You know, you can use that muse thing all you want, but I still don't buy it," she teased him.

Branch shrugged as he took another bite of his burger. "Okay, even though it's true that you are my muse, I'll put it this way. I'm glad I went to the cemetery tour—and I skipped my evening workout to go to it, by the way. But I'm glad I went. Otherwise I would never have met the woman of my dreams."

Tansy's heart leapt in her chest. *That* was what she wanted to hear! Oh, it was flattering, wonderful, and very romantic that Branch claimed she was his muse—that his inspiration had excelled since he met her. But to hear him say that she was the woman of his dreams? It was perfect!

Still, she knew propriety, if nothing else, begged that she play at disbelieving. Therefore she said, "Wow! You're good!"

Branch's eyes narrowed as he looked at her, and his intense, provocative gaze caused such a thrill to travel over her spine that she actually felt her insides quiver for a moment.

"Oh, you have no idea," he mumbled. "I'm keeping my most serious thoughts to myself…so you really have no idea."

Tansy felt her cheeks warm with a delighted blush. "I'm beginning to think you're a wolf in sheep's clothing, mister."

Again Branch shrugged, saying, "All men are, Tansy. In one way or the other."

"Is that so?" she giggled.

"Okay," he said, tossing the remains of his burger onto his plate and thoroughly wiping his hands on the napkin he then wadded up and tossed onto the plate as well. "You want the truth?"

"Always," Tansy assured him.

Branch looked at her, stared at her with such a lack of joviality in his expression that Tansy was half afraid he was going to confess to stringing her along just to find out more about Sleepy Hollow. But what he said took her breath away.

"I'm gonna marry you, Tansy Sheridan. I mean, if you want the honest truth...I knew it the minute I first saw you. I knew the other night, when I took that first tour through the cemetery, that you were the one. And I'm not kidding, and I'm not feeding you a line. So there you have it." He paused, his expression still entirely serious, even severe, and then he asked, "So...what say you to that, apple tree girl?"

But when Tansy opened her mouth to speak, she found that the only thing that came out was a stammering, "Well, I...I...I..."

With an emphatic nod of having been proven right about something, Branch said, "That's exactly what I thought you'd say." He exhaled a heavy sigh. "That's why I've been keeping my thoughts to myself, because I knew you'd think I was crazy...or a player at the very least."

"But I don't!" Tansy exclaimed. Desperate that Branch understand that she was just as crazy as he was—that she'd loved him from that first night in the cemetery as well—she began to babble, "I feel the same way! I just thought...well, I *knew* you'd think I was some desperate, whacked-out, psycho stalker girl like you see on cop shows or read about in books, you know? I mean, I've known you, what? Not even forty-eight hours yet? But I *feel* like I've known you my whole life! I have the freaked-out fear that I'll wake up in the

86

morning and find out this was all a dream…or that you really are a player and once you get all the info you can from me to work on your book, you'll just up and go back to wherever you came from without one final word or anything!" She reached out across the table and took one of his hands in hers. "I mean, *I* think I'm crazy…so why wouldn't you think I'm crazy, you know?"

Branch studied her for a moment. Then, very slowly, a rather triumphant grin began to spread across his handsome face.

He exhaled another heavy sigh, this one an obvious sigh of relief. "I was afraid you were going to stand up and start screaming for the cops as you ran out of here as fast as you could," he admitted.

"No," she told him. "Not at all."

Pulling his hand from hers, Branch smiled as he reached around, retrieving his wallet from his pocket. "Well, I'm ready to get out of here *with* you," he said.

Taking a couple of twenties from his wallet, he tossed it onto the table, returned his wallet to his pocket, and slid out of the bench.

"What do you say we just get out of here and find a place where we can be alone and…and talk?" he asked, offering a hand to her.

Nodding with exuberance, Tansy took his hand and allowed him to pull her out of her seat and to her feet. Still clasping Tansy's hand, Branch practically dragged her from Hathcock's and out onto the sidewalk.

All of a sudden, Tansy found herself enveloped in Branch's powerful embrace. She gasped with surprise as his mouth claimed hers in a very possessive, very intimate kiss—right there on the sidewalk in front of Hathcock's! It seemed he didn't care one bit about who might see him kissing her. And although the kiss was not incredibly long, it *was* incredibly passionate—incredibly rapturous—purely incredible!

"I was afraid you were going to tell me to get lost," he said once he'd broken the seal of their mouths.

"Oh, like any woman in all the world would ever tell *you* to get lost," Tansy teased.

"Quit trying to make me feel better about turning into a lovesick puppy when you showed up in my life," he chuckled.

Tansy bit her lip with the wonder she was feeling as she gazed up into Branch's eyes—his gorgeous green eyes that were simmering with affection, with passion, with emotion, and all of it directed at her.

She knew there were all kinds of things that would work against their whirlwind romance. He lived in Texas, and she lived in Sleepy Hollow. Her parents—his parents—what would they think? Would their families try to discourage them from being together? Try to convince them there was no possible way two people could fall in love in less than forty-eight hours?

But Tansy didn't want to think about the challenges that might face them—not yet, anyway. At that moment, she simply wanted to think about being with Branch Jackman forever.

Branch was gazing at Tansy as well, but when he glanced up for a moment, a frown puckered his brow.

"What the hell is that?" he mumbled.

Tansy looked over her shoulder a moment—unwillingly released her embrace of Branch and turned to see what he was frowning at.

"Oh, that," she said when she saw what had captured his attention. "That's something they do around here every autumn—you know, just to make things fun and to supply photo opportunities for tourists and stuff."

Branch's eyebrows arched as he continued to stare at what was coming down the street toward them. "Wow! That looks totally legit," he commented.

Tansy smiled as she watched the Headless Horseman astride a large black horse, racing down the middle of the street in their direction.

"I know, right?" she agreed. "The Headless Horseman guys around here take the role very seriously. Nothing cheap or unprofessional when it comes to the Headless Horseman in Sleepy Hollow, you know?"

"You'd think this guy would be more careful with the fire though," Branch mumbled. "I mean, the jack-o'-lantern he's holding is flaming pretty intensely. It looks almost a little too legit."

Tansy felt a slight frown pucker her own brow then. Branch was right; the flaming pumpkin this particular Headless Horseman was carrying did indeed look a bit too flaming. Seeing a Headless Horseman riding through the streets of Sleepy Hollow wasn't at all an unusual sight. Tansy had seen them many, many times—at least two or three times a year ever since she could remember. But what she did not remember was seeing a Headless Horseman riding as fast as this one was—at a speed quite unsafe for any pedestrians that might not be paying attention—and carrying a jack-o'-lantern that was flaming so apparently out of control.

As usual, tourists and locals alike stopped dead in their tracks or looked out from restaurant or shop windows to watch the dramatic display. But when Tansy felt Branch take hold of her arm and begin to pull her further back from the street, she did not pause—for this Horseman had an air of malice preceding him. For the first time in her life, Tansy was fearful of one of Sleepy Hollow's Headless Horsemen.

Everyone standing around watching was wowed into either awed silence or applauding appreciation—but not Tansy. And when the Horseman reared his black horse in the street directly before the place where Tansy and Branch were standing, she felt a sort of panic rise in her.

The Horseman's costume was superb—the best Tansy had ever seen, and she'd seen a great deal of incredibly authentic-looking ones. His black cape billowed out in the breeze, and his black boots and gloves looked to be real leather and very worn. The Revolutionary-era breeches, shirt, and coat he wore under his cloak were definitely high-end as well. Yet Tansy did not recognize the man's costume at all. Furthermore, there were so many black horses kept by locals for just the purpose of dressing up like Irving's infamous Horseman that she couldn't begin to tell to whom the horse belonged.

The Horseman pulled his horse into a rearing position for a moment, brandishing the flaming jack-o'-lantern high above him, and every witness lining the street gasped with admiration at the menacing display.

Instinct drove Branch to take hold of Tansy's arm and pull her to stand behind him. Headless Horsemen riding out at night around Sleepy Hollow may have been commonplace enough, but Branch sensed this was not the average Sleepy Hollow Joe out and about simply to entertain tourists.

And, as always, Branch's instincts were correct—for as soon as the black horse had finished rearing and stood firmly on all four legs once more, the apparently headless man astride him reeled back, launching the flaming pumpkin directly at Branch. He raised his arm in time to feel the pumpkin hit his forearm with tremendous force but was thankful he'd managed to deflect the flaming projectile from hitting Tansy.

"Hey, man!" he shouted, striding out into the street to confront the Horseman. "What the hell are you doing? You could've hurt someone!"

"Dude! You're on fire, man!" someone yelled from behind him.

"Branch!" he heard Tansy scream.

It was only then that Branch realized the jack-o'-lantern the Horseman had thrown must've had some sort of accelerant inside it. A faint whiff of kerosene filled his nostrils as he looked down to see that the sleeve and most of the side and back of his shirt were on fire.

Angry that the rogue Headless Horseman could've easily set Tansy on fire instead of himself, Branch ignored the thought to stop, drop, and roll and simply tore his shirt off, discarding it on the ground as he continued to stride toward the villain on the horse.

"Get off that horse! Now!" he shouted. He was infuriated beyond any infuriation he had ever known. This guy had tried and almost succeeded in hurting Tansy—and Branch meant to beat the hell out of him!

The Horseman, however, had different ideas. A moment before Branch reached him, the troublemaker turned his horse and rode off at a full gallop in the direction from whence he'd come.

"Dude! Are you all right, man?" a guy about Branch's own age said as he jogged up to meet him. "Maybe you should go get checked out at the hospital," the man suggested.

"Branch!" Tansy cried as she ran to him.

She was sobbing as she threw her arms around him, hugging him so tightly around the waist he had a hard time drawing a deep breath.

"I'm fine, baby," he soothed, kissing the top of her head as he wrapped her in his arms. "Are you okay?"

Taking her face in his hands, he forced her to look up at him—studied her tear-stained face in searching for any sign of injury she may have sustained when the flaming pumpkin shattered on his arm.

"I'm fine, you stupid, dumb man! I'm fine!" she cried. "But you…you were on fire, Branch! On fire!"

"Somebody should call the cops," the guy who'd first approached Branch shouted.

The night lit up as everyone began calling and texting on their phones.

"Branch?" Tansy whispered, reaching up to take Branch's face in her hands. "Are you really okay?"

Branch liked the way his face felt under her touch—the warmth, the softness of her palms and fingers against his skin.

Smiling at her, he reassured, "I'm fine. Really. But I'm going to need a new shirt."

Tansy forced herself to smile as she gazed up into Branch's ruggedly handsome face. He'd been on fire! How could he joke about it? And yet he was all right—seemed completely unscathed. So she wrapped her arms around him again, pulling herself tight against the warm, smooth contours of his chest and stomach.

"Wow," she breathed as he held her, kissed the top of her head, and stroked her hair with reassurance. "You're really muscly, you know? I never knew illustrators were so ripped," she teased.

"Well, you never know when some freak is going to throw flaming pumpkins at your girlfriend, right? A guy's gotta be prepared," he told her.

In a mere matter of moments, lights and sirens arrived.

As Officer Van Tassel got out of his unit and walked to where Tansy and Branch stood on the sidewalk, he shook his head.

"Didn't I just talk to you two last night?" he asked, reaching out to shake Branch's hand.

"Yes, sir," Branch assured him. "I guess someone has it in for Tansy. She nearly stumbled into an open grave last night, and then tonight this guy rides up and throws a flaming pumpkin at her head."

"Well, the legend does say that the Headless Horseman needs a new head and..." Tansy began.

"Not funny," Branch said, tucking her protectively under his arm and placing another kiss to the top of her head.

Officer Van Tassel shook his head. "What's going on, Miss Sheridan?" he asked.

Tansy shrugged. "I don't know," she answered. "I don't think it's really anything involving me. I think it's just my being in the wrong place at the wrong time."

Officer Van Tassel and Branch exchanged expressions of doubt. "It's too coincidental to my way of thinking, Miss Sheridan," Officer Van Tassel said. "I'll take your statements now, but I think you should come down tomorrow morning and have a sit-down with us at the station, okay?"

"But—" Tansy began.

"You too, sir," Officer Van Tassel said to Branch. "It could be you're the focus as well."

"But...I'm not even from here," Branch pointed out.

"That's exactly why I think you better come in too. Something's up...and it's just too strange that you two have been at the center of it both times. All right?"

"Okay," Branch and Tansy responded in unison.

"For now, let's just get your statements and get you guys on your way. We'll be sure to interview other witnesses too," Van Tassel explained.

"Tansy!" Jeanna Sheridan called out at she hurried toward Tansy.

"Mom?" Tansy asked as her mother hugged her. "What are you doing here?"

"I was in town to pick up some fabric from the shop, and I heard all the commotion," her mother explained. "Then I look over here to see you in the center of everything…cops everywhere." Jeanna paused, looked to Officer Van Tassel, and said, "Hi, Louis. What on earth is going on?"

"I'll let your daughter explain everything, Jeanna," Van Tassel said.

Jeanna looked at Branch then. "And what on earth are you doing outside this time of year with no shirt on, Mr. Jackman? You'll catch pneumonia!"

Branch raked a strong hand back through his hair. "Well, my shirt caught fire and—"

"Mom, just let us go talk to the police, and then we can tell you everything, okay?" Tansy interrupted.

"Well, maybe not everything," Branch told Tansy in a lowered voice.

Tansy smiled at him, delighted with his flirting. Her heart was still racing with the residue of fear, panic, and relief that Branch was all right. But his flirting did soothe her somewhat.

"All right," Jeanna said, exhaling a sigh of impatience. "But hurry up, Tansy. I'm a nervous wreck now."

"Okay, Mom," Tansy said.

"Actually, Mrs. Sheridan," Branch began, "we might be a few minutes. So if you feel comfortable with it, why don't you head home, and Tansy and I will follow as soon as we're finished here. Would that be all right? I was planning on driving her home anyway, and I'd like to be involved in explaining everything...if that's all right with you, that is."

Tansy smiled when her mother arched one eyebrow. It was her mother's expression of suspicion, and Tansy knew it well. Still, Jeanna Sheridan smiled, nodded, and halfheartedly agreed, "Well, all right. But hurry up. I'll be a nutbag until you get home safely, okay?"

"Okay, Mom," Tansy said, returning her mother's embrace.

She smiled when her mother wagged an index finger at Branch, saying, "You better just bring your PJs and plan on staying the night with us, Mr. Jackman. I have a feeling you'll be there pretty late explaining all of this, hmmm?"

"Yes, ma'am," Branch said without pause. "Whatever you say, Mrs. Sheridan."

As her mother walked away, Branch smiled down at Tansy. "Looks like we're having a sleepover at your mom's house, hmm?"

"Har har," Tansy said—though his flirting caused butterflies to erupt in her stomach. Branch Jackman was going to take her home to her parents' house and stay the night? It was too delicious for words!

As Tansy stood listening to Branch give his statement to one of the police officers, she studied him at her leisure. Dang! He was ripped! She'd always heard that farm boys were well built, but heck! This guy was like a Roman god or something! Tansy didn't spend a great deal of time thinking about muscles—washboard abs, giant biceps, and broad shoulders. But the truth was, she didn't think anyone would linger around Branch when he was wearing boots, jeans, and no shirt and *not* be lost in admiration.

She kept thinking of how wonderful his skin had felt against her cheek when she'd had her face pressed to his chest—of how his kiss intoxicated her limbs and made every nerve in her body tingle. She also kept thinking of how much she liked talking with him, being with him, sharing stories and meals with him. In truth, Tansy knew that even if Branch Jackman weren't built like a Roman god and more handsome than any man who'd ever worked in Hollywood, she'd still be in love with him. She giggled to herself, however, as she inwardly admitted that she was glad he looked like a Calvin Klein men's underwear model all the same.

CHAPTER SEVEN

"Well, I think Louis Van Tassel is grasping at straws," Joel Sheridan said.

"It is kind of weird, Joel, don't you think?" Jeanna asked as she poured more orange juice into his glass.

Tansy and Branch were sitting at the kitchen table having breakfast with her dad and mom. The night before had been eventful to say the least. Yet Tansy found that even the crazy Headless Horseman throwing a flaming pumpkin into a crowd of onlookers hadn't done anything to taint the memory of the glorious day spent with Branch. If nothing else, it was like an exclamation point at the end of a beautifully written sentence. And watching him as he sat at the table wearing Star Wars pajama bottoms and ratty white T-shirt (the PJs he'd stopped at his hotel and grabbed at Jeanna's request) was like the icing on the cake.

Branch's hair was tousled, giving him the look of a groggy little boy—and he was adorable! He was enjoying one of her mother's delicious omelets, and Tansy was glad her mom had supersized it—

for she knew that even a supersized Jeanna Sheridan omelet wouldn't last Branch more than two hours.

"Yeah, it is," Tansy's father answered her mother. "But Sleepy Hollow is a small town. And this time of year, most out-of-towners can be found congregating at restaurants, the cemeteries, and all the other popular sites any time of day or night. So I wouldn't put too much worry into Louis taking every precaution and interviewing these two just in case. It's good police work."

Tansy grinned when she looked up at her father to see him wink at her conspiratorially. She knew he was trying to ease her mother's mind. And anyway, she figured he was probably right.

"After all, Mom, it's not like I'm the type to attract a stalker or anything," Tansy offered. "And Branch has only been in town less than a week, so he's certainly not a target. We're about the only ones who know him." She smiled, adding, "Well, us and Mrs. Sturbridge over at the historical society. I mean, she did let Branch rummage around in the back rooms for hours…all by himself."

Jeanna paused—the spatula filled with the omelet she'd been about to put on her husband's plate hovering over the skillet she held in her other hand—and Joel's eyebrows raised as they both stared at Branch in disbelief.

"Mirna Sturbridge let you into the back rooms?" Jeanna asked in a squeaky voice that revealed just how astonished she was.

"Mirna?" Joel inquired as well. "Tall, skinny old bat with gray hair and trifocals? That Mrs. Sturbridge?"

"Yeah…" Branch slowly answered.

Tansy giggled. "I told you, Branch. Mrs. Sturbridge doesn't take to anybody!"

"And she certainly doesn't let anyone into the back rooms—ever! And never on their own!" Jeanna stated as she finally slipped the omelet from the spatula onto Joel's plate.

"What the hell is going on here?" Devon asked as he entered through the back door that emptied into the kitchen. "The guy gets one pumpkin tossed at him, and now he's Mom's new baby, or what?" Smiling, he offered a hand to Branch, chuckling as he said, "What's up, man? I hear the Headless Horseman went after your head last night."

Branch stood up, grasping Devon's hand and giving it a firm shake. "Something like that, I guess."

Kyle stepped through the door and into the kitchen next, adding, "Well, I guess he finally found a head as handsome as mine then. He's been after me for years." He shook Branch's hand as well and then sat down at the table across from Branch.

"You boys want omelets this morning?" Jeanna asked as she kissed each of her sons on the cheek.

"I already had a big breakfast, Mom. Thanks," Devon answered.

"I'll take one, Mom," Kyle said.

"So you've already heard about the pumpkin thing last night?" Tansy asked her brothers.

"Oh yeah!" Devon said. "It's all over town—how the Headless Horseman tried to decapitate some tourist with a flaming jack-o'-lantern. It's in the morning paper and everything."

Branch grinned, looked to Tansy, and said, "Hey! We made the paper! Cool."

"And only a day after you about fell into old lady Van der Veen's grave too, huh, Tanz?" Kyle teased.

"You heard about that, huh?" Tansy said. "Poor Anouk Van der Veen," she sighed. "I feel so bad that she was disturbed. And I'll never get that image of that stake pounded down right in the middle of her out of my mind."

"Cool!" Kyle and Devon said in unison.

"You boys be nice," Jeanna scolded, thumping each of her sons on the back of their heads with the handle of her spatula. "Your poor sister has had a rough couple of days."

"A rough couple of days?" Kyle exclaimed. "Hanging out with some famous artist dude, happening upon open graves, nearly getting tagged by the Headless Horseman? She's livin' large, Mom!"

Everyone laughed—everyone but Jeanna. "Well, I don't think nearly getting burned to death is livin' large." She looked to Branch from where she stood in front of the stove. Shaking her spatula at him, she said, "I'm just glad you didn't suffer any serious burns, Branch."

"Me too, ma'am," Branch admitted. Scraping his plate with his fork, Branch ate his last bite of omelet. "I guess I better get dressed so we can head down to the police station, right?" he said to Tansy.

"Yeah," Tansy agreed. "There are towels in the hall linen closet there, and you can just use the bathroom near your bedroom if you want to shower."

"Thanks," Branch said. Pushing his chair away from the table, he stood. "Thank you for the wonderful breakfast, Mrs. Sheridan. That was the best omelet I've ever had…really."

Jeanna smiled with delight. "You're welcome, Branch. I'm so glad you enjoyed it."

Branch looked to Tansy again, saying, "I'll be fast." Then he nodded to each of her brothers. "See you guys later." He offered a hand to her father, and Tansy smiled as her daddy wiped his mouth with his napkin before standing to shake Branch's hand. "Thanks for letting me bunk over for the night, Mr. Sheridan. I slept like a rock."

"Anytime, Branch," Joel said.

Once Branch had left the room, Devon and Kyle began pummeling Tansy with questions. She silently hoped that Branch really would be fast—because she didn't feel like lingering with her smart-aleck brothers right then. She felt like being with Branch—and only Branch—even if it was because they had to go to the police station for a more intensive discussion with Officer Van Tassel. At least it was time spent in Branch's company. And spending time in Branch's company was all Tansy ever wanted to do again—ever!

♥

"We identified the horse as belonging to Archer Van Buskirk," Officer Van Tassel explained. "He said he didn't even know it was missing until he went out to feed it this morning. Whoever stole it just let it go after the incident last night."

"Wow!" Tansy breathed. "So other than that—knowing that whoever that was last night stole a horse—it's still a total mystery, huh?"

"I'm afraid so," Officer Van Tassel admitted. "But it helps that you two came in this morning. It sounds to me like both of you were just in the wrong place at the wrong time…twice."

"Stranger things have happened, I guess," Branch said. Then offering his hand to Officer Van Tassel, he added, "Thanks so much, officer."

"Thank you, Mr. Jackman," Officer Van Tassel said as he shook Branch's hand. He looked to Tansy then, nodded, and said, "Even though it doesn't seem like these two things have anything to do with you, Miss Sheridan, please do be wary. My gut tells me this is the same person, and I'm not sure how determined he or she might be where malicious intent is concerned."

"I will," Tansy assured him. "I mean, I suppose if it were just the grave thing, you could chalk it up to somebody just messing around. But Branch could really have been hurt last night. Anybody could've."

"Exactly," Officer Van Tassel agreed. "That's why I'd rather you two be safe than sorry, you know?"

Both Tansy and Branch nodded their reassurances that they would be careful.

Tansy exhaled a heavy sigh as she and Branch left the police station. Her time with Branch was over, and she felt entirely drained, unmotivated, and even discouraged.

"Well, I guess I'd better get back to work," she said, turning to face Branch. She smiled as he immediately drew her into his arms.

"Me too," he mumbled into her hair before kissing the top of her head. "Although I'm not sure I'm going to be able to concentrate on sketching anything but you today. So maybe I'll just check out the housing market around here…being that I'm going to need a permanent residence here in Sleepy Hollow now."

Gasping with excitement, Tansy looked up at Branch, asking, "You're going to move here? Really? You're really going to move to Sleepy Hollow?"

Branch smiled, an amused chuckle rumbling in his chest and throat. "Well, if I'm gonna marry you, I have to be where you are, where your apple trees are…just in case you ever do get that Harrison apple tree graft one day, right?"

Instantly Tansy felt tears brimming in her eyes. Was he serious? Would he really give up his home in Texas—living so close to his own parents and where he was born and raised—just to be with her? Was it possible that he truly already understood how much she loved the orchards and her work in trying to save vanishing varieties of apples? It seemed so silly when she thought about it—her love for apples and the trees that bore them. At least, it seemed silly when compared with the way she felt about Branch.

"You know that I'd move to Texas instead, don't you?" she ventured. "I...I would never ask you to leave your family and—"

"I have a gift, Tansy," Branch explained. "It's a gift a lot of people don't have, and that is that I somehow can kind of figure things out ahead of time, you know? Like, of course I love Texas and I love my family, but my work...I can do that anywhere. Literally. Your passion for saving apples, caring for the orchards...that can't just pick up and move. And besides, I can see how close you are to your parents, even your brothers. I know you'd come with me to Texas. But I can already tell you that our life together will be better here." Branch shrugged and casually added, "So I'm just going to find a permanent residence—or at least semi-permanent...because I'm hoping you'll chose to live with me after we're married and not on your own or with your parents."

Tears were rolling down Tansy's face in streams—or at least it felt that way. She couldn't believe what he was saying. He meant to move to Sleepy Hollow? They'd known each other—what?—three days, and they were already talking about when they were married? Were they crazy?

"Do you think we're crazy?" she asked out loud in a whisper.

Branch grinned, brushed a strand of hair from her cheek, and said, "I think our souls recognized one another the moment we met, and we just need to trust them." He laughed, adding, "We're not crazy, but I guarantee you everyone else will think we are. So I hope you're ready to dig in for the fireworks."

Tansy brushed at the tears on her cheeks as she nodded. "I am. And besides, we can just act like we're working up to it for a while, right? No one has to know that—"

"Will you marry me?" Branch asked. "I mean, when the time is right…will you?"

He was proposing? Tansy couldn't believe it! And yet as her heart leapt with overwhelming joy and assurance inside her bosom, she answered, "You bet!"

She was in Branch's arms then, held tightly in the strength of them as he kissed her. Right there in front of the Sleepy Hollow Police Station, Branch kissed her with such fervor Tansy thought she might faint from pure elation! His mouth was warm and moist as he worked such a spell of pure, bewitching passion over her that her arms and legs went numb all at once.

Tansy had never been a fan of public displays of affection—at least not ones that appeared to be as passionate as the one she and Branch were sharing felt to her. But she didn't care. She didn't care if Officer Van Tassel himself strode out of the police station and issued them some sort of citation. She was going to kiss Branch as long and as thoroughly as she wanted to!

Their kiss was interrupted, however, not by Officer Van Tassel but by Mr. Brenden.

"Oh, Tansy! I'm so glad to see you!" a very winded Mr. Brenden said.

"Mr. Brenden? Is everything all right?" she asked. Certainly she was disappointed that her moment with Branch had been interrupted. Yet Mr. Brenden looked quite disheveled and out of breath.

"I can't get into the receiving vault at the cemetery," he said. "I've got to get in there and set up things for the tour tonight, and I can't find my key anywhere. Marvin isn't answering his phone. But when I saw you and your friend here...well, I was wondering if you still have that extra key I gave you a couple of weeks ago."

Tansy smiled, exchanging relieved and understanding glances with Branch.

"I do have it," Tansy assured him. Reaching into her pocket, she pulled out her keys. "I'll just give it to you, and then you won't have to worry."

Mr. Brenden chuckled. "As relieved as I am that you have it, would you mind keeping it until mine shows up...or Marvin does, at least? It's the only other spare I have, and I don't want to risk misplacing it. We've got a couple of really big crowds scheduled for some of the tours tonight, and I'd hate any of the groups to miss the finale at the vault." Mr. Brenden looked to Branch. "I heard about what happened last night, so I know you both must be tired. But would you mind just running over to unlock the vault for me, Tansy? Bring your boyfriend here too. I just need to get into that vault to prep things."

Tansy liked the fact that Mr. Brenden recognized that Branch was her boyfriend. And she liked that he, in a roundabout way, was asking Branch to allow him to inconvenience them so he could get into the vault.

"I'll be happy to let you in, Mr. Brenden," Tansy assured her friend. "You don't mind, do you, Branch?"

Branch smiled at her—smiled lovingly at her—and it hatched a million butterflies in her stomach.

"Not at all," Branch answered. "We can't have the finale of the cemetery tour being messed up. It's the best part!"

Mr. Brenden straightened his posture with pride. "Thank you," he said to Branch. "I try to make it special."

105

"And you succeed," Branch assured Mr. Brenden.

As the three of them began walking toward the cemetery, Mr. Brenden frowned and said, "I haven't been able to get ahold of Marvin all this morning. He was supposed to be at the cemetery at nine a.m. to begin grounds maintenance, and when he didn't show up…well, he always calls in if he's sick. He left work early yesterday too. Do you think I'm being overly concerned?"

"That does seem odd," Tansy said. "Even for Marvin," she giggled.

Mr. Brenden smiled and chuckled a bit. "Yes, it does."

"But I'm sure he just overslept or something," Tansy suggested.

"That's probably it," Mr. Brenden agreed. "He'll probably show up later today with some cockamamie excuse, right?"

"Right," Tansy agreed.

"So," Branch began as they neared the cemetery, "how long have you been working with the cemetery tours, Mr. Brenden?"

"Oh, years and years now," Mr. Brenden said.

Tansy smiled at Branch—her silent thank you to him for being kind to the old groundskeeper.

In a matter of minutes, they'd reached the cemetery, and as they walked toward the receiving vault, Mr. Brenden prodded Branch. "Mrs. Sturbridge tells me you're working on a graphic novel of the legend of Sleepy Hollow. Is that right?"

"Yes," Branch answered. "I'm also working on illustrations for a children's edition of the story."

"Well, it might interest you to know that many of my ancestors are buried right here," Mr. Brenden bragged. "It's very important to me that everything concerning Sleepy Hollow is portrayed correctly…and with respect."

Branch looked at Tansy, and both raised their eyebrows to indicate that they knew they had better say just the right thing or risk offending Mr. Brenden.

"You wanna go ahead and unlock it for me please, Tansy?" Mr. Brenden said, nodding toward the two iron gates that were the entrance to the receiving vault.

"Of course," Tansy said.

In truth, the receiving vault creeped her out even in the daytime. The large gray stone edifice, where the dead were once stored in horizontal brick crypts during winter months when the ground was too frozen to dig a grave, simply seemed like the stuff of horror movies. No wonder movie producers used the spot on occasion to film.

As she put her key into the lock of the gate, however, Tansy frowned. "Mr. Brenden," she began, "it's not even locked. Did you check it before—"

It was the sound of something falling to the ground that caused Tansy to whirl around. And it was the sight of what had fallen to the ground and why that caused her to gasp in fear—caused her heart to leap up into her throat with trepidation and terror.

For there stood Mr. Brenden, a crowbar in his hand. And at his feet lay Branch—his eyes closed, his body lifeless.

CHAPTER EIGHT

"Branch!" Tansy cried. Yet as she began to lunge forward toward Branch, Mr. Brenden brandished the crowbar higher above his head.

"Calm down, Tansy," Mr. Brenden said. "Just calm down. He'll be fine. When he wakes up, he'll just have a little bump on his head."

Fearful of the crowbar Mr. Brenden was wielding, Tansy stopped in her tracks. "You might have killed him!" she screamed. "Have you lost your mind?"

At that very moment, Tansy heard a muffled cry. Glancing to Branch to see that he still lay unconscious, or perhaps worse, at Mr. Brenden's feet, she was momentarily confused.

"You see?" Mr. Brenden said then. He smiled, adding, "Marvin's fine. He's been in there all morning, and he's fine."

Horrified as she realized that it was indeed Marvin calling for help from somewhere inside the receiving vault, Tansy shook her head, looking to Branch as tears streamed down her face.

"Mr. Brenden, what is wrong with you?" she asked. "Let me just go to Branch. Let me just make sure he's all right."

Mr. Brenden shook his head, however. Then as he hunkered down, placing a hand on Branch's back, he said, "See? He's still breathing. He's fine—just unconscious for a little while. And this actually worked out better than I thought." As a smile of triumph spread across his face, the man said, "Now there will be three of you in the vault when the tour groups go through tonight! Everyone will be terrified!"

Tansy knew she had to keep her wits about her. If Branch was going to get help, if Marvin was ever going to get out of one of the tombs in the receiving vault, she had to keep as calm as she could.

"Ah ah ah," Mr. Brenden warned. Smiling at her as if he'd just read her mind, he said, "Don't try to run, Tansy. You wouldn't want your young man here waking up inside his tomb to find that you'd run away and left him to entertain the guests with just Marvin alone, now would you?" Standing to his full height once again, he took a step toward Tansy. "Now, if you just cooperate with me, Tansy, I won't have to knock you over the head too. Just get into one of the tombs, and let me seal you in there—just until after the tours tonight—and then I'll let you out…Marvin and your boyfriend too. But we need to have people understand how important Sleepy Hollow is, how valuable its history is. And don't you think that making the tour as realistic as possible will help with that?"

"Mr. Brenden, please…" Tansy began.

But Mr. Brenden's smile had faded, and as he took another step toward her, Tansy saw the hatred in his eyes. "Mrs. Sturbridge told me everything—how this guy you've fallen for is planning on publishing a graphic novel about Sleepy Hollow, planning to make our town, our legend of the Horseman, everything…he's planning on mocking it, lessening its value and importance by creating a glorified comic book about it. And a children's edition?" He shook his head with disgust. "Our history—Mr. Irving's profound telling of Sleepy Hollow—it's not meant to entertain children."

"Mr. Brenden," Tansy ventured, "Branch doesn't plan on disrespecting anything about Sleepy Hollow or the legend of the Headless Horseman. He's only—"

"He's an outsider!" Mr. Brenden shouted. "He doesn't appreciate our history. Why, so many of us have roots reaching back to the founding of this town—especially me! My ancestors were among the first Dutch settlers to arrive here, and I won't have their hard work, their patriotism…I won't have it reduced to a comic book!"

Tansy was trembling with fear and anxiety. Marvin's cries from within whatever tomb Mr. Brenden had walled him up in were growing panic-stricken. She could hear him beating on the stone that covered the opening to his tomb. Far more horrifying was the fact that Branch was lying facedown in the grass, blood oozing from a wound at the back of his head. Tansy had no way of knowing how badly he was injured. Mr. Brenden had proved that Branch was still alive—Tansy could see his back rising and falling with his rhythmic breathing—but that didn't mean he was out of danger. She didn't know what to do! If she tried to scream or run for help, she might end up with the crowbar smacking her across the back of the head as well, and then she'd be of no use to Branch or Marvin. Yet she certainly wasn't going to climb inside one of the vault tombs and allow Mr. Brenden to wall her up inside—her or Branch.

As more tears began to spill from her eyes—as Mr. Brenden took another step toward her, still wielding the crowbar in a menacing manner—Tansy glanced to Branch once more. She held her breath as she saw his eyes open. They were barely open—no more than narrow slits—especially at first. But then full consciousness seemed to wash over him with a wave of adrenalin.

Tansy gasped as she watched Branch leap to his feet. Lunging forward, Branch grabbed Mr. Brenden around the waist, pushing him to the ground.

"Get on the ground!" Branch shouted. "Get on the ground!"

Mr. Brenden tried to struggle. But he was no match for Branch, and in mere seconds, Mr. Brenden lay flat on his stomach, rendered entirely helpless as Branch forced his arms to his back, holding the backs of his hands together, bent at the wrists so that he couldn't possibly escape.

Shaking his head in an obvious attempt to dispel the dizziness that no doubt still had his senses whirling, Branch looked up to Tansy from his place straddling Mr. Brenden's body.

"He's a total nut job," he growled. "Run back to the station and grab some cops, Tansy," he almost ordered. "I'll wait here."

"But are you…are you all right?" Tansy cried. She wanted to run to him, fling her arms around his neck, and kiss his mouth in knowing he was alive and would be well.

"I'm fine. But try to hurry," Branch answered. "I've got a killer headache. And I think someone is locked up back in that vault too."

"It's…it's Marvin," Tansy stammered, brushing tears from her cheeks.

"Oh, then…you better hurry," Branch said. He shook his head again, and Tansy knew Branch was not out of the woods yet. "I'll be fine until you get back." He forced a reassuring smile, adding, "I promise. Just hurry, okay?"

Tansy didn't speak another word, simply nodded and began running as fast as she could through the Sleepy Hollow cemetery and toward help—help for Branch.

♥

"Looks like you had a nice takedown on that guy," one of the police officers told Branch.

Branch was sitting on the back bumper of the ambulance as an EMT inspected the wound on his head.

"I guess all those episodes of *Cops* I've been watching my whole life finally paid off," Branch chuckled. "At least I didn't get walled up in some ancient tomb like that guy," he added, pointing to where several other policemen stood talking with a very pale and rattled Marvin.

The police officer nodded. "Yeah. That's gonna haunt him for the rest of his life, no doubt about that."

"Are you sure you're all right, Miss Sheridan?" Officer Van Tassel asked for the tenth time. "You've been through a lot these past couple of days."

"I'm fine. Really," Tansy said, even as more tears brimmed in her eyes. "I-I just can't believe it…all of it," she admitted. She looked up at Officer Van Tassel. "You were right. It was *us* that started all of this with Mr. Brenden."

"It was mental illness that caused all this, Miss Sheridan," Officer Van Tassel firmly stated. "Everybody in town knows that Brenden has always been a little too eccentric when it comes to Sleepy Hollow. And it seems that eccentricity just finally jumped to mental illness. He says he dug up that grave the other night to get people's attention. Apparently even local citizens were stopping by the historical society to get more information on the history of the woman buried in a porcelain coffin with her emeralds." Officer Van Tassel shook his head. "Well, in the end, I suppose he's going to get what he wants…more attention for Sleepy Hollow."

"Okay, I'm fine," Branch said, obviously having spent as much patience as he could being fussed over by the EMTs.

"You really should go to the hospital and have a doctor examine you more thoroughly, Mr. Jackman," a pretty brunette EMT suggested with a smile.

"I will, I will," Branch assured her as he stood.

Not pausing another moment, he reached out, gathering Tansy into his arms.

"I've never been so terrified in all my life. When I woke up and saw that idiot standing over you with that crowbar, I couldn't believe it," Branch mumbled into her hair as he repeatedly kissed the top of her head.

Tansy clung to him desperately, her tears moistening the front of his shirt. "I thought you were dead," she sobbed for a moment. "I thought he'd killed you!"

But as Branch stroked her hair and kissed the top of her head, she could hear the strong beat of his heart inside his chest where her head pressed against him, and she was reassured that he was well.

"We're both all right," he said as if reassuring not only her but also himself. "We're both all right."

"Tansy!"

Tansy pulled back from Branch just a little when she heard her mother's voice.

"Tansy! Are you okay?"

Branch released her as both her mom and dad arrived, her mom claiming Tansy in her own embrace.

"Baby girl, are you okay?" Jeanna asked, holding Tansy at arm's length and studying her face.

"I'm fine, Mom, really," Tansy said. "It's Branch that we need to worry about."

"You all right, son?" Tansy heard her daddy ask.

"Yes, sir," Branch said.

"Louis called us right away, and we got here as fast as we could," Jeanna explained. She shook her head with disbelief. "To think that Mr. Brenden would do something like this! I…I just can't believe it."

"Oh, he's always been a nutbag, Jeanna," Joel grumbled.

"Well, yes, we all know that, Joel," Tansy's mother grumbled back. "But I don't think anybody ever would've guessed he was this crazy."

"He's been dating Mirna Sturbridge for ten years, Jeanna," Joel added. "We should've known just by that."

Tansy smiled as she hugged her dad. She loved the way he always managed to diffuse sad or dramatic situations with his sense of humor.

"I oughta gut that man myself for trying to harm you, baby girl," her father whispered into her ear as he hugged her.

"I love you, Daddy," Tansy breathed as tears filled her eyes again.

When Tansy pulled back from her father, it was to see her mother fussing over Branch as if he were a wounded puppy.

"Now you're sure they checked you out thoroughly, honey?" her mother asked Branch. "I don't want you having a concussion and—I don't know—having brain damage from it or whatever comes with concussions."

"I'm fine, Mrs. Sheridan," Branch said, smiling with appreciation at her concern—as well as amusement.

A sudden breeze puffed by, sending fallen leaves whirling at everyone's feet. The aroma of warm bread fresh from the oven wafted from the bakery, and even for the bright sunshine of midmorning, the cool, crisp atmosphere of autumn caused Tansy to shiver.

"I'm definitely moving here," Branch said, taking Tansy's hands in his own and kissing her squarely on the mouth.

Tansy giggled when she saw both her parents staring with mouths agape and eyebrows raised in astonishment.

"Did…did you say you're moving here?" Jeanna Sheridan asked.

Branch nodded. "Yep. Before all this mess interrupted the morning, I was on my way to look for a house."

"You like Sleepy Hollow that much?" Jeanna asked, eyebrows still arched in awe.

"I like your daughter that much," Branch answered plainly.

"So…am I to understand you're planning to move here for Tansy?" Joel asked. His expression of astonishment slowly turned to a frown of concern.

Branch winked at Tansy, in letting her know he knew her parents were about to freak out, a moment before he said, "Well, I can't very well get to know Tansy better if I'm clear out in Texas all the time. So being that I can work from anywhere and that I find my inspiration really seems to have come alive here…yep, I've decided to move to Sleepy Hollow."

Tansy's mother smiled at her—winked with understanding—and Tansy knew her mother truly did understand. After all, her mother had always claimed that she knew Tansy's father was the only man for her the moment she first saw him. So it made sense that her mother would be less concerned than her father. That, and the fact that Tansy's daddy was always very protective of his daughters.

Tansy watched as her father inhaled a deep breath, seeming thoughtful for a moment. "Well, I guess we'll see what happens then, hm?" he mumbled. "Meanwhile, we better run you on over to the hospital and make sure your noggin is all right on the inside."

Tansy glanced up to Branch, hoping that he would read her mind and know that it was important to her father that Branch agree to be examined more thoroughly.

"Yes, sir," Branch said, winking at Tansy.

Branch held Tansy's hand as they walked to her parents' double-cab pickup. Her mother was insisting her father drive them all to the hospital—that Branch shouldn't be driving after a head injury.

Lowering her voice, Tansy asked Branch, "Are you sure you don't want to just escape back to Texas? They can be kind of bossy…especially once they start considering you one of their kids."

Branch chuckled. "I get the same thing from my parents, don't worry."

"So even after getting hit over the head, you still plan on moving here and…you know, where I'm concerned, you still plan on…" Tansy stammered.

"Marrying you?" Branch finished for her.

"Yeah," Tansy answered. She found she was holding her breath, worried that he might actually have changed his mind.

"More than ever," he assured her, however. Then leaning over to whisper in her ear, he added, "The hard part will be waiting for the realization to sink into your parents' heads, you know?"

Tansy nodded.

"I figure I'll wait two weeks before asking your dad for permission to marry you," Branch said. "Hopefully I can win him over by then."

"You won him over the instant you won me, Branch," Tansy said. "And you won me the moment I first saw you."

"Not even three whole days ago," Branch added.

"Yep. Not even three whole days ago," Tansy confirmed.

"I love you, Tansy," Branch said, tucking her under his arm as they walked. He kissed the top of her head, sending warm delight racing through her body.

All her life, Sleepy Hollow in autumn had always been enchanting for Tansy. But now she knew that *this* autumn—the autumn that brought her romance, the autumn that brought with it her one true love—this autumn would forever be the most enchanting of all.

EPILOGUE

"Mmm!" Branch said as he kissed Tansy's neck. "You smell like apple pie."

Tansy turned in her husband's arms. Lacing her fingers at the back of his neck, she said, "Well, you smell like handsome!"

"You can't smell handsome," Branch chuckled.

"You're my husband. I can smell everything about you," Tansy teased. "I can smell that you're handsome, that you're so talented you've been commissioned to illustrate three—count 'em, three—fairy tales and two DC Comics. And most of all, I can smell that you've been working in the orchard this morning."

"Really?" Branch said, raising one arm to sniff his armpit.

"Yes—because you smell like apple trees, not sweat, dorkus," Tansy giggled.

Branch placed a moist, lingering kiss at the hollow of Tansy's throat. "Mmm. I think smelling like apple pie is so much better though. I could just eat you up, Tansy Jackman."

Taking Tansy by the waist, Branch lifted her onto the kitchen counter and proceeded to bless her with a delicious, very impassioned kiss.

Tansy was awed with the way Branch's kisses always weakened her knees, even after almost a year of marriage. Butterflies still fluttered madly in her stomach when he did—goose bumps still raced over her limbs—and she knew they always would when he kissed her the way he was kissing her now.

"I have some more news for you, baby," Branch mumbled against her mouth.

"And what might that be?" she asked against his.

"*October Calls Her Name*," Branch answered. "I sold it…for a mint."

"What?" Tansy exclaimed. Placing her hands on his shoulders, she pushed Branch back to stop him from kissing her again. "What do you mean, you sold it?"

October Calls Her Name was a painting Branch had finished in February—just two months after they were married. It was a painting of Tansy dressed in the historic garb she'd been wearing during the Sleepy Hollow cemetery tour when she and Branch first met. The cemetery itself was the scene—ancient trees dripping with gold, orange, and red leaves, tombstones that were hundreds of years old dotting the foreground. It was both beautiful and haunting—and Tansy loved it!

"You sold my painting?" she asked as tears began to fill her eyes.

"Oh no, baby, not the painting itself," Branch assured her, realizing that she was upset. "I sold the rights to print it—to allow one art company to sell copies of it, babe, that's all," Branch explained, gathering her into his arms. "You know I'd never sell the real thing."

Tansy choked back the now unnecessary tears and sighed, "Oh, whew! For a minute, I thought you'd lost your marbles."

Branch smiled. "Nope. Not at all."

"I love that painting!" Tansy continued. "I always like to think that when you first saw me in the cemetery…well, that you saw *only* me, like in the painting. It's kind of my stupid fantasy thing, you know? That you fell so instantly in love with me, it was as if there were no other people around for miles."

Branch smiled and kissed her again. "It's not a fantasy, Tansy. That is exactly how I remember that night. I really don't remember anybody but you in that moment. I know there was a whole group of people, but when I think about it—when I look back and remember it—all I see is you."

Tansy caressed her husband's handsome beyond handsome face as she gazed into his dazzling deep green eyes. "That's how I remember it too. Only you…no crowd, not Marvin or Mr. Brenden dressed up like ratty old Barnabas Collins…just you. You took my breath away that night, you know?"

"Oh, I'll take your breath away right now, my little apple pie," Branch said as he swooped Tansy off the counter and into his arms.

Tansy giggled with delight. Branch was so romantic!

"Promises, promises," she teased.

As Branch began racing down the hallway toward their bedroom, he said, "I told your dad I'd be back right after lunch…but what's he going to do if I'm late? Fire me?"

Tansy laughed as Branch tossed her onto their bed.

"Are you really mine?" she asked as he hovered over her—the promise of passion in his smoldering gaze.

"Are *you* really *mine*?" he asked in return.

"Forever and ever," Tansy whispered as Branch brushed a strand of hair from her forehead. "And ever and ever and ever..." she repeated until his mouth capturing her own hushed her.

AUTHOR'S NOTE

Remember last year when I wrote *Romance at the Christmas Tree Lot*? Well, as I began writing *this* book, knowing it would also be a novella, I thought, "Why not call it *Romance in Sleepy Hollow*? And why not write a novella now and then with a title that begins *Romance at the…* or *Romance in…*?" So, yes! Before I even begin this trivial little author's note, I'm revealing that I do plan to write some more *Romance…* novellas over the next few years! I hope that comes as a pleasant announcement to you, knowing that there will be some more lighthearted stories like this one.

Meanwhile, back at the ranch, one of my very favorite quotes is this one by George Eliot (a.k.a. Mary Ann Evans): "Delicious autumn! My very soul is wedded to it, and if I were a bird I would fly about the earth seeking the successive autumns" (October 1, 1841). It is just such an expression of how I feel about autumn. I swear to you that I long for autumn all the months of the year that are not autumn! I can't wait for that one morning, usually about mid-August here in New Mexico, when I step outside and can feel "it," as my daughter and I refer to the slightest change in the air that lets us know autumn is arriving. It's exactly as if my soul is set free on that day every year when "it" shows up one morning—and my entire being is happier from that day until December 26, when I start longing for autumn again.

I'm sure you've already figured out that, in wanting to linger in autumn a little longer this year, I sat down and treated myself to a little autumn romance—and here it is! I know that *Romance in Sleepy Hollow* won't change your life—because it wasn't meant to. It's just a little autumnness for you to linger in with me, while I wait for that day in August next year to kiss my cheek with its crisp, cool promise that autumn has come to make my heart happy again.

As Ever, Yours,
Marcia Lynn McClure

Snippet #1—My bedroom is decorated in exactly the same manner as Tansy's—from the autumn quilt to the art on the walls, the candle votives, and even the first line of "Autumn Leaves" in vinyl lettering adorning one wall so that it's the first thing I see in my room each morning. I even have a wooden plaque hanging over our bedroom door as you enter; it reads, "An Autumn Haven." Yep, I'm that autumnally obsessed!

Snippet #2—My "Autumn Leaves" Playlist—If you'd like to slap together a playlist or CD featuring some of my favorite renditions of "Autumn Leaves," here's a list of the ones I have on my playlist. It's wonderfully calming when you're feeling like you need a break—especially in autumn (of course, ha ha!).

"Autumn Leaves"—Bing Crosby

"Autumn Leaves"—Newell Olar

"Autumn Leaves"—101 Strings Orchestra

"Autumn Leaves"—Jo Stafford

"Autumn Leaves"—Paul Desmond

"Autumn Leaves"—Nat King Cole

"Autumn Leaves"—Simply Clarinet

"Autumn Leaves"—Frank Sinatra

"Autumn Leaves"—Vince Guaraldi

"Autumn Leaves"—Matt Monro

"Autumn Leaves"—Johnny Mercer

"Autumn Leaves"—Roger Williams (I'm not real fond about the beginning but like the rest)

"Autumn Leaves"—Chet Atkins

"Autumn Leaves"—Richard Hayman

Snippet #3—Tansy's Brothers' Names—Devon and Kyle, Tansy's two older brothers, were inspired and named after two teenaged boys of our family's acquaintance. You've already been introduced to Kyle (Max-slash-Kyle from the author's note of *Midnight Masquerade*). And now you've been introduced to Devon, Kyle's older brother. If there are two boys who have bright eyes that are always, *always* filled with mischief, it's Kyle and Devon! Both boys (ages fifteen and thirteen at this point) are diehard Batman fans, and this year for Christmas I decided to make them Batman pillowcases to enhance the giant bags of teriyaki jerky Kevin and I will give them as their Christmas gifts. Well, the other day, I was in the fabric store and saw this fabulous Wonder Woman fabric. Being that I immediately thought of these two mischievous brothers and their admiration for Batman, I grabbed a couple of yards of voluptuous Wonder Woman fabric and made two Wonder Woman pillowcases to go with the Batman ones. Ah ha ha ha! I can just see their faces when they lift out the Batman pillowcases to see the voluptuous Wonder Woman ones underneath! They'll be embarrassed beyond explanation—mortified! Touché, right?

Snippet #4—The Graveyard Tour of 2006—In June of 2006, our family was on a work retreat kind of thing with the company Kevin worked for at the time. One of our family's favorite moments of all of the places we visited—Plymouth Rock, Cape Cod, New York, etc.—was the nighttime Ghost and Graveyards Tour in Boston. It was awesome, and I based my version of the Sleepy Hollow cemetery tour (which they really do have, as well) on my own experience in Boston. I *loved* that tour! And as in the tours Tansy helped with, there were people hidden here and there throughout the cemeteries that would suddenly appear in period clothing and looking like ghosts and tell the tour group wonderful historical accounts of the lives of some of the people interred the cemetery. One lady ghost even took a liking to my youngest son, Trent, chasing him around one cemetery, in and out of the tombstones as she tried to steal a kiss! It was horrifying for him—being that he was, like, twelve and nowhere near being ready to handle the affections of a lady ghost in a cemetery. But all in all, our family loved the tour! I'd like to visit some other historic cities and take their cemetery tours one day—especially Sleepy Hollow's!

Snippet #5—Interesting Speculation about Irving's Katrina Van Tassel—From what I've read concerning the Sleepy Hollow cemetery in New York, both Catriena Ecker Van Tassel and her niece Eleanor Van Tassel Brush are buried in the Sleepy Hollow cemetery, and it has long been proposed that one or the other, or perhaps both, contributed to Washington Irving's inspiration for Katrina Van Tassel in his story "The Legend of Sleepy Hollow." Just a little fun fact I came across while researching that I thought I'd pass along to you.

Snippet #6—I *do* collect children's books! And you may or may not have known that already. However, what you probably don't know is that one of my favorite children's authors is Cynthia Rylant. She's marvelous! I just love the *feel* of her books. Somehow she manages to sweep me away to a space of tranquil serenity, and I love her for that. All of her books are wonderful—either fun, charming, or simply beautiful—but I've decided to list a few of my favorites, in case you're looking for something to read to your children (or to yourself) that weaves a peaceful, comfortable, and sometimes lulling-to-sleep mood.

The first book by Cynthia Rylant that I ever read I stumbled across over twenty years ago, and it's still fun for me. It's entitled *The Relatives Came* and is a fun, sentimental read about the excitement of a group of favorite relatives coming to visit from afar. In truth, I don't know if most of us visit like this anymore—you know, where we bunk in with each other and just have ridiculous fun hanging around. Still, it's one of my favorites of Cynthia's, so give it a try!

Her book entitled simply *Snow* is one of my favorites as well. Talk about a lulling-to-sleep book! It's a very soothing book, perfect for wintertime just before bed. *In November* is a beautiful autumn/winter book too—another favorite. I've gifted both *Snow* and *In November* to friends more times than I can count!

Night in the Country and *Christmas in the Country* are two that I love. *Let's Go Home* and *The Blue Hill Meadows* are darling! And there is a series of books called the Cobble Street Cousins, the first of which is entitled *Aunt Lucy's Kitchen*, that are adorable.

Cynthia does have a few more melancholy books as well, just as a heads up. Although I did enjoy her *Children of Christmas* book—a collection of six stories that portray a wide variety of "moods"—it wasn't a happy, happy, joy, joy book. But it was still so beautifully written and incredibly affecting that I truly loved it anyway.

So there you have it—Tansy and I both collect children's books! And, in truth, I *so* wish an illustrator the likes of Branch Jackman had illustrated a book titled *October Breezes*, written by an author the likes of Cynthia Rylant. Can you just imagine?

Snippet #7—The Flashlight in the Latrine—Branch's experience with accidentally dropping a flashlight down the latrine at summer camp is actually based on the real-life experience of my youngest son, Trent. Branch's illuminated latrine story is exactly Trent's—even the part about his worrying that his mom had spent a ton of money on the flashlight. The true story of Trent, summer camp, his flashlight, and the latrine still makes my heart ache when I think about it. My poor son, so worried over a flashlight the whole time he was at camp that year. It makes me tear up to think that the whole thing caused him such intense anxiety. Of course, now—years and years later—we all have a great laugh over the whole illuminated latrine thing. The light from the flashlight really did last through two full nights, shining up from the depths of the latrine sludge, through the seat hole, and out of the latrine like a beaming beacon. Those were some great batteries, I guess.

Snippet #8—Stop and Smell the Horse Manure?—Over twenty years ago, I was browsing through a craft store (the kind where people sold things they'd already made, not the Hobby Lobby kind) when a little framed quote caught my eye. The matting surrounding the quote in the frame was your typical colors so popular in the early to mid-'90s—forest green and burgundy—but the quote was not so typical. In fact, I've never seen it anywhere since. Inside the beautifully '90s matted oval were the words, "You've got to stop and smell the horse manure!"—and I loved it instantly! The handwritten quote (handwritten in beautiful calligraphy, mind you) seemed as if it had been written just for me. I mean, "Stop and smell the roses" is what we've all been told and heard. And yes, it's a very important piece of advice. But to me—well, roses shmoses! Stopping to smell the horse manure makes so much more sense to me! My rural background, my love of all things old-fashioned, and my fond memories of farm life meant that stopping to smell the horse manure was something I truly understood! In truth, it's dairy cattle cow manure that I prefer; that aroma of chewed, coughed-up, and rechewed alfalfa is mellow and sweet. Nothing like the stinky, stomach-wrenching stench of feed-lot cattle cow manure. I'm sure you know what I mean. But horse manure has a charm all its own as well, and although a framed quote of, "You've got to stop at the dairy barn and smell the cow manure," would've pleased me even more, I was perfectly delighted with "You've got to stop and smell the horse manure." It spoke to me, you know? I knew exactly what the person who had crafted the little framed quote to sell in her craft booth meant. It's somewhat akin to my favorite H.D. Thoreau quote—the one that hangs above the toilet in my guest bathroom— "I'd rather sit on a pumpkin and have it all to myself than be seated on a velvet cushion." Both of these quotes remind me to take the time to enjoy the beauty of nature, the wonder of memory, and to be ever thankful for the simple things in life. For in truth, the simple things are the profound things, you know? The quiet peace of standing in a pasture or out on the mesa—the sight of a field of pumpkins off in the distance—horse manure dappling the trail alongside a riverbank. All these things are food for the soul. Money and things, social position and popularity—they weigh us down. But horse manure? It takes us back to simpler times—to the smell of saddle leather and oats—to grandpas that could do anything and grandmas that could ride as well as any cowboy ever did. When it comes to stopping to smell something that makes a body feel peaceful and appreciative of life itself, I'd choose horse manure any day over roses!

Snippet #9—My Favorite Story—You may or may not already know this, but Washington Irving's short story "The Legend of Sleepy Hollow" is my very favorite! It's so beautifully written. The descriptions of that part of the country in that time period are incredible! And Irving's way of sparking your mind's eye and imagination are just too wonderful to be missed. Although I've loved the story since I was a child, I was in my forties before I ever read the real, unabridged (although very short) version of "The Legend of Sleepy Hollow." That's probably a good thing, for I'm not sure I would've had the appreciation for the way Irving wrote, let alone the time alone to really concentrate on it, when my kids were little or even when I was a teenager. So even though this novella is just a little fun piece to help us all escape life's stress and demands for a few hours, I hope that it inspires anyone who reads it to pick up "The Legend of Sleepy Hollow" by Washington Irving and give it a try.

But wait until October one year—because it's extra wonderful to read it in October. I love October!

My everlasting admiration, gratitude and love…
To my husband, Kevin…
My inspiration…
My heart's desire…
The man of my every dream!

ABOUT THE AUTHOR

Marcia Lynn McClure's intoxicating succession of novels, novellas, and e-books—including *A Crimson Frost*, *The Visions of Ransom Lake*, *The Bewitching of Amoretta Ipswich* and *Midnight Masquerade*—has established her as one of the most favored and engaging authors of true romance. Her unprecedented forte in weaving captivating stories of western, medieval, regency, and contemporary amour void of brusque intimacy has earned her the title "The Queen of Kissing."

Marcia, who was born in Albuquerque, New Mexico, has spent her life intrigued with people, history, love, and romance. A wife, mother, grandmother, family historian, poet, and author, Marcia Lynn McClure spins her tales of splendor for the sake of offering respite through the beauty, mirth, and delight of a worthwhile and wonderful story.

BIBLIOGRAPHY

A Bargained-For Bride
Beneath the Honeysuckle Vine
A Better Reason to Fall in Love
The Bewitching of Amoretta Ipswich
Born for Thorton's Sake
The Chimney Sweep Charm
Christmas Kisses-Three Favorite Holiday Romances
A Crimson Frost
Daydreams
Desert Fire
Divine Deception
Dusty Britches
The Fragrance of her Name
A Good-Lookin' Man
The Haunting of Autumn Lake
The Heavenly Surrender
The Highwayman of Tanglewood
Kiss in the Dark
Kissing Cousins
The Light of the Lovers' Moon
Love Me
The Man of Her Dreams
The McCall Trilogy
Midnight Masquerade
The Object of His Affection
An Old-Fashioned Romance
One Classic Latin Lover, Please
The Pirate Ruse

The Prairie Prince

The Rogue Knight

Romance at the Christmas Tree Lot

Romance in Sleepy Hollow

The Romancing of Evangeline Ipswich

Romantic Vignettes-The Anthology of Premiere Novellas

Saphyre Snow

Shackles of Honor

The Secret Bliss of Calliope Ipswich

Sudden Storms

Sweet Cherry Ray

Take a Walk with Me

The Tide of the Mermaid Tears

The Time of Aspen Falls

To Echo the Past

The Touch of Sage

The Trove of the Passion Room

Untethered

The Visions of Ransom Lake

Weathered Too Young

The Whispered Kiss

With a Dreamboat in a Hammock

The Windswept Flame

www.ingramcontent.com/pod-product-compliance
Lightning Source LLC
Chambersburg PA
CBHW072028170626
46811CB00008B/2989